GONE WOMAN

A.J. RIVERS

PROLOGUE

"Behind Blue Eyes"

FADE IN:
EXT. LANDSCAPE – DAY, EARLY MORNING

Open with a sweeping shot of the land. The field is empty; the grass tipped in dew. Pre-dawn blue atmosphere. Move to the garden, the stables, and finally, a golden dirt path.

VIOLET: (V.O.)

There are some things your mother never teaches you. One of them is how to die.

CUT TO:

INT. – SHADOWY LIGHT – TIGHT SHOT OF WOMAN'S FACE
Sound of fast, shallow breathing. Blue eyes snap open.

———

He made sure her eyes were open. That wasn't a mistake he was going to make this time. He'd been fooled by the first woman. Her closed eyes had seemed appropriate, but they'd concealed the tightness of her stomach muscles as she held her breath and the fluttering of her rapid heartbeat just beneath the surface of her summer-gold skin. He'd come to hate that skin. Perhaps that's why he didn't notice her struggle to conceal that little bit of life still left in her. He couldn't bring himself to look at her that closely anymore. Her clumsy bolt through the house, the last bid for survival, had been an inconvenience he'd rather not repeat. Chasing her had left troublesome blood drops across the white carpet. It had taken all night for him to wash them away, and even still, two days later, they rose up from the fibers again. Fainter, but there. So, he'd cleaned again. He couldn't have it like that when his new wife came home. She would notice.

But he had learned from that mistake. He ensured this woman's eyes were wide open. Much simpler. They were still visible through the clear sheeting. Three large rose bushes sat in the grass behind him, ready to mark and conceal the ground where he would lay her. Perfect white blooms. That's all he wanted. Crisp, clean perfection. It's why she tumbled into the ground now. It's why another would follow.

She wasn't missed yet, but soon she would be.

By then, he'd have what he'd always wanted.

Cool white light replaced the burning glow of day overhead. He pushed the rolled sleeves of his white shirt higher over his elbows and filled the shovel with the first scoop of dirt. It rained down over her, and he couldn't help but wonder what she would see if those wide eyes were watching.

CHAPTER ONE

MARY

I brace myself against the intense cold as I run through the deep snow. It's biting, the wet chill sinking through my clothes and onto my skin. My legs ache, the muscles feeling as though the individual fibers have turned to ice and are slicing through the veins and skin around them. I look down at them. I'm not wearing enough clothing for the intense cold swirling around me. My skirt brushes my knees, exposing a long stretch of skin above my lightweight shoes. My skin looks pale and sparkles with flecks of snow that tumble through the air around me. Each breath cuts through my lungs and hangs in opaque white gusts in front of my mouth.

Every step is excruciating, but terror keeps pushing me forward. I don't know where I'm going or what I'm running from. Whatever it is, it's close enough behind me to keep the hair on the back of my neck standing up and my legs pumping. The swirl of the snow keeps getting thicker the further I go. Trees on either side of me block my view, and something tells me if I can just get past them, I'll find safety.

I think I hear my name echoing through the cold. But maybe that wasn't it. It sounded familiar, and it didn't. The sound could have just as easily been the call of a night bird as it could have been a voice. But I haven't heard any other birds. There is only the sound of my footsteps crunching over the snow. I try to think it through, to figure out how I got here, what drove me into the blizzard when I'm obviously not prepared for it. But I can't drag anything forward. All that exists in my mind is fear.

Finally, just ahead of me, I see the end of the tree line. The space is bright white and glittering. If I can just make it through the blackened skeletons of trees, I can get away. Every breath is getting more difficult. It feels like less and less oxygen is getting into my lungs as I inhale the snowflakes and let them build up in icy drifts inside me. My fingers ache, and strands of my hair feel heavy and brittle hanging against my wind-battered cheeks.

Something – or someone – is coming after me. They're getting closer. The whipping, rippling air cascades the snowflakes around me. Each is its own sound. A screech of wind. A note of music. A syllable of my name. As they stream past my face and cling to my skin, they bring the sounds with them until they are as disorienting as the whitewash and the cold.

I could duck behind one of the trees and hide. But then what? I don't know what's behind me or what it's seen. Even if hiding confused it, the cold would take me within minutes. Running keeps my blood from freezing and forces it through my veins. It's all that's keeping my body warm. If I crouch down behind a tree, I'll be buried in the snow. Forgotten.

Just get beyond the trees. If I can get there, I'll be safe.

Finally, I break beyond the tree line. The fear still creeps up the back of my neck, but there's a timid, cautious sense of hope as I run out into the open space. Even the snowflakes were lessening, like I'd willed them to quiet, like I'd earned the softer brush of them against my skin.

The lift of hope is short-lived. The heavy snowfall meant flakes stinging in my eyes, blurring my vision. Gone now, I can see ahead of me. In the distance, there is... nothing. Where there should be more openness, more snow, there is only a strange shimmer. The air itself seems to have captured the light from the ice and is reflecting it back.

Beyond that is darkness. I run to it, hoping it will disappear. Instead, I see myself.

A shadowy, translucent image of my own wild eyes and tangled hair, my frozen blue skirt and ice-coated legs, comes toward me. I'm emerging from the darkness toward myself, and new fear wraps my stomach around my spine. The closer I get to the shimmering air, the farther I watch myself run back toward the trees.

I stop, and my image stops. The strange, glistening mirror image is less than a foot in front of me. My hands tremble as I lift them. The hands that match mine feel cold and hard. A reflection in the glass trapping me.

The tears on my cheeks sparkle like the snow.

———

Warren Hull's voice snaps me out of the disturbing vision, startling me so much I nearly drop the snow globe in my hand. Gripping it tightly to compensate for the way my hand is still shaking, I carry the decoration over to the mantle and nestle it amongst the shiny green holly boughs. A quick brush of my dusting cloth takes away the prints my fingertips left. Laughter from the audience trickles from the television in the corner, and I cross the room to turn it off. Time got away from me while staring at the globe. I didn't realize it was already past eleven-thirty.

I never watch *Strike It Rich.* Those people are so desperate for help, and the television producers trot them out to be a spectacle for people sitting at home watching. Thank goodness the weekly evening version stopped airing in January. And yet, somehow having it show at this time of day makes it worse. Housewives have enough on their mind taking care of their homes and their families to be drawn into the tales of woe the contestants tell. Especially at this time of year. Christmas is just two weeks away, and watching those sad-eyed people hoping for the scraps of help the show can give could make anyone feel guilty about decorating their home and preparing gifts.

The distinct *click* of the dial sends the house into silence. A chill ripples down my back. I'm used to being home alone while Charles is at work, but there are days when the silence is unnerving. It moves through the house, filling the rooms, and leaving me waiting to hear... something. That uncertainty of what I might hear brings me over to the radio. Another dial clicks, and Bing Crosby melts away the silence.

It's impossible not to feel the spirit of the holidays when listening to his voice. Humming along, I open the next of the boxes stacked neatly in the corner. The smell of last year's Christmas wafts out at me. It's a smell that never changes. Cinnamon and paper, pine boughs, and gingerbread. Dust and cardboard. Breathing in memories. I only wish I could make them more real.

Charles came home with our tree a few days ago and then dutifully went to the attic to bring down the boxes. He's strung the silvery green branches with lights, but the rest of the decorations are still tucked away. We'll trim the tree together. But for now, there are plenty of other touches I can put on the house. Starting with the pictures of us from past years. I set the silver frames on the mantle, focusing on the pictures rather than the snow globe between them. The first picture is of Charles and me standing beside a far sparser tree than the one we have now. White lights make it seem to glow and cast shadows over us. But through the dimness I can see Charles has his arm around my waist, and my head leaning toward his as I smile up at him.

"That was one of our best Christmases."

I gasp and turn around, pressing my back to the fireplace and my hand to the center of my chest. Charles crosses the room to me quickly, his eyebrows furrowing with worry.

"Charles," I force over my erratic heartbeat.

"I'm sorry, Darling. Did I startle you?"

He brushes his thumb over my cheek. His voice is smooth like Bing Crosby's.

"I didn't hear you come in," I tell him.

"It's noon," he says. "I told you I'd come home for lunch. Or did you forget?"

Something flickers in the back of my mind, and I wrap my arms around his neck for a hug.

"Of course, not," I say, even though I had. "I must have just gotten so wrapped up in preparing for Christmas."

He smiles at me, and I feel a familiar brief sense of relief when he steps away from me. I hate that relief. But it's there.

"You always have."

I step out of the intensity of his gaze to turn back to the picture.

"When was this?" I ask.

He steps up beside me, and I feel the warmth of his hand on the small of my back. Holding me steady. Guiding me.

"Five years ago," he explains. "Our first Christmas in this house. You were so excited to get our tree; you insisted we go out on Thanksgiving to get it." He chuckles in a way that sounds like it's rattling around in a can. "Of course, none of the lots were open Thanksgiving night, but for you, Darling, I will find anything."

"Even a Christmas tree on Thanksgiving night?"

He touches his finger to the glass over the tree.

"After driving around from lot to lot, I finally stopped at a little farm out past the edge of town. There were some trees growing around, and I walked right up to the front door, knocked on it, and asked to buy one."

I feel like I should laugh, but the sound won't form in my chest. This isn't a story; it's a lesson.

"You didn't mind bothering them on the holiday?" I ask.

"It was for you. When I left the house that night, you were already preparing the living room. I wasn't going to come home without a tree for you. So, I marched right up to the door, determined to fulfill my promise. The man who answered wasn't happy with me, I'll tell you. But I told him it was for my bride and that softened him up. He sold me a tree and a length of rope to tie it to the roof of the car, and I brought it home. It wasn't until I got it here and brought it inside that I realized it was the scrawniest tree I ever did see."

His laugh rattles a little less this time. It tugs the corners of my lips, encouraging the smile that should be there. I turn back to the picture and let my eyes scour it. They dig into the shadows and plunge past the hazy needles. Searching for something. Anything that feels familiar beyond the story. Charles has told me that story before. I've seen other pictures and prepared the corner of the living room the same way for this tree as for that. But those are his words. I want to find something in the picture that's mine.

"I just wish I could remember."

CHAPTER TWO

MARY

"I know, Darling." Charles takes my wrist and pulls me away from the mantle and my search. "You will. More has been coming back every day. Just like the doctors promised."

Rudolph crackling over the radio feels invasive.

"You must be hungry. Let's have lunch."

There used to be a window over the sink. I suppose it's still there. The sill still juts out from the creamy wall, and the wooden frame still sketches out the shape. But the pink curtains hang over a smoothly painted piece of wood sealed into place over the glass. It's been that way for as long as I can remember. And as long as I can't.

Last night's roast beef makes perfect sandwiches on the loaf of stiff sourdough Charles brought home from the bakery. Alongside deviled eggs I made this morning and a scoop of the macaroni salad always sitting on the bottom shelf of the refrigerator, it doesn't seem I forgot about him coming home. It's just a simple lunch, so we eat at the pink Formica table in the kitchen rather than going to the dining room. He takes a bite of his sandwich, and his eyes drop to the empty spot by the top of his plate.

He doesn't say anything. He doesn't have to.

"What are you planning for this afternoon?" Charles asks as I start a fresh pot of coffee.

"I thought I would start addressing the Christmas cards," I tell him.

My husband nods approvingly.

"I'll leave my address book for you."

"Thank you."

The smell of coffee bubbling through the percolator takes the place of more words. His deviled egg is gone, and most of his macaroni has joined it by the time I set a white mug of black coffee beside his plate.

"Is something bothering you?" he asks after a few more minutes when he notices my sandwich hasn't moved, and my egg has just made a slight turn across the plate.

I know I shouldn't bother him. He's been working so hard recently, and I know he's gone through so much for me already. But his dark grey eyes don't move away from me. Even as I take a sip of my own milk-swirled coffee. Even as I swallow a bite of cold roast beef.

"It happened again," I tell him.

His hand comes across the table to touch mine.

"Another vision? What did you see?"

"The woods. I don't know where. I was running."

"Running?"

"Something was chasing me."

"An animal?"

"I don't know."

These are my words, the only ones I really have. So much has slipped through my fingers, I don't know what to think or to trust. Not until I hear my own voice say it.

"Darling, I'm worried about you. These visions have been happening more often. I can see how much they upset you. You really should talk to the doctor about it."

I shake my head adamantly.

"No," I say. "Please don't ask me to do that."

"It's really concerning me. I thought your visions would get fewer with time and you'd get more of your memory back, but it's been six months since the accident."

"I know."

"The doctor may be able to help you. Don't you want to stop seeing these things? Don't you want to remember our life together?"

"Of course, I do. But if I have to go to the doctor…"

Charles knows what I mean, even without me finishing the sentence. Seeing a doctor would mean going out of the house, something I haven't done since the day we moved in. Agoraphobia seals me into this house. It set the wood into place over the windows and built up the stone breezeways leading from the doors to other doors. All designed, so I don't see the world beyond the house, a world that makes my stomach turn and my heart pound just thinking about it. Designed to make me feel safe.

Of the few memories I grasp, the clearest ones are of that world. They are little more than flashes, but they are visceral and terrifying. A sharp, medicinal smell burns in my nose and creates a metallic taste down the back of my throat when I breathe. Hands grab me, moving me onto a hard, rolling table. Bright lights explode against my eyelids. When I think of them now, I know they were trying to save me. It still makes my throat tighten and my heart pound in my ears.

"You know I'll always keep you safe," Charles says. He glances down at his watch. "I tell you what. I'm going to call the office and tell them I won't be able to come in for the rest of the day. That way, I can stay with you."

"Oh, you don't have to do that," I say.

Even as I say it, I hope he stays. Having him here with me leaves less room for the silence.

"Yes, I do, Darling. I can see how shaken up you are. We'll decorate together, and I can do some work here while you do the Christmas cards."

I nod as he stands and leans down to kiss me on the top of the head. He leaves the kitchen to head for his den while I clean up the dishes. There's enough coffee in the percolator to top off his cup, so I fill it and carry it to the den. I can hear Charles talking as I walk down the hallway.

"I'm sorry to hear that. Don't give up hope. You know how women can be. With Christmas coming, I wouldn't be surprised if you came home from work and found her in the kitchen making fudge like nothing has happened."

The conversation piques my curiosity, but I don't linger in the hallway. I don't want him discovering me out here and thinking I'm eavesdropping on him.

I'm back in the living room with the boxes of Christmas decorations giving off their scent from years past when Charles comes in. He's slipping his coat on over his suit and has his hat gripped in one hand.

"I'm sorry, Darling," he frowns. "Work is too busy this afternoon for me to not be there. Since we're breaking soon for Christmas, we want to get as much done as possible before then, and they don't think they can handle it without me."

A dial clicks inside me. I offer him a smile.

"That's because you're so important," I tell him. "Of course, they can't get on without you."

Charles grins and crosses the room to me. His hands feel strong on my hips, like they're both holding me up and keeping me in place. He kisses me quickly, rethinks it when his lips are barely off mine, and dips down for a longer, softer one.

"I won't be late," he promises. "After supper, we'll get that tree decorated and see if there's a Christmas special on the television so we can cozy up and watch it together."

"That sounds nice."

"Good. Be brave, Darling. Everything is alright. Spend some time really looking at the Christmas things. Maybe it will bring back some memories for you."

Adjusting his hat in place, Charles lifts the collar of his coat to protect his neck from the cold and gives a final wave before leaving the house. The shutting of the first door tells me he's gone. The second reminds me I'm alone. Perry Cuomo's crooning brings an unexpected sting of tears to my eyes.

There's no place like home for the holidays...

CHAPTER THREE

CHARLES

The front door closing sounded loud against the still quiet of the early afternoon. Charles stepped out onto the front porch and adjusted his hat. Light glinted through the window of the house across the street, reflecting off the bright tinsel draped over the branches of their Christmas tree. At exactly six that night, the multi-colored bulbs would pop on. It was steady and predictable, exactly as he liked it.

He looked out over the lawn. Each blade of grass was exactly the right length, but there was something off. It angled his face down and dampened the spirit brought on by the music and the decorations. Crossing the yard, he reached down and gathered the dried leaves from beneath the rose bushes. Once satisfied by the neatness of his yard again, Charles climbed into his powder blue car and broke the winter silence with the roar of the engine before driving out of the neighborhood.

The drive to the office was only a few minutes, and he hummed a Christmas carol to himself as he drove. All around him, the holiday season was in full force. Lights strung across the street waited for illumination when evening would fall. Houses had been neatened up, and candles burned in some of the windows. Only a few more days of work, and then he'd be able to retreat home and enjoy the rest of the season with Mary.

A young man he had recently hired waved at Charles from across the parking lot as he pulled into his designated spot. He didn't remember his name. His role was small, and he'd only be around for a few weeks, so Charles didn't feel the need to learn much about him. As the man paused to open the door for a secretary going inside, Charles committed the image to mind. Maybe he would take note of the young man's name and contact information. If he does well in this position, he might have more opportunities in the future.

Water glasses and stacks of paper cluttered the large, long table as Charles walked into the conference room. The rest of the team looked up at him with the weary eyes of men who'd taken their lunch in the building. They were ready to break for the holiday season and take some time away from this project to breathe. It had been a long and challenging experience so far. Unexpected delays, legal threats, and major changes to the original plans meant stretched days and count-less mugs of coffee. But it was coming together. Soon he'd have what he'd been working toward for years.

"Good afternoon, gentlemen," he said as he hung his coat on the rack and dropped his hat on top. "How was your lunch?"

There were a few half-hearted responses, but his smile didn't waver. Charles couldn't help but feel for the men flanking the long brown table who didn't have what he did. A few of them brought lunches their wives packed for them. Others ducked over to the diner not far from the office to pick up a sandwich or, if they were lucky, a box of fried chicken. None went home to wives waiting to prepare their lunch and give them a break in the middle of the day.

He was a lucky man.

"Lovely," Daniel Pierce said to his left, pushing past the topic and moving on. "We finished those interviews."

"Great. How did they go?" Charles asked.

The LB Project was his passion project. Filling the gap left by the woman who walked away months before had been a frustration he'd be glad to have over.

"We've shortlisted six for the next steps," Pierce continued. "All but two agreed to come back next week."

"Then you've shortlisted four."

"It is the holidays," Gregory Harmon pointed out from the other side of the table. "They didn't want to say no but had already made plans to travel to see their families. In any other circumstances…"

"Well, this is not 'any other circumstances'," Charles said firmly. "This project has already been delayed enough. If the candidates are not able to fulfill the requirements, they are no longer qualified. You should be happy about that. It simplifies the process. We just went from six options to four. When that's finished next week, we'll be another step closer to finally getting this finished. Now, update me on the progress of the rewrite."

Papers shifted across the table, and several of the men took turns speaking. Their words piled up on top of each other, each of them offering pieces of a larger picture that gradually fit in around each other. The final image was forming. It had already been finalized once before. At least, Charles thought it had been. Clear and precise, it was the vision he'd carried for years. Until it suddenly changed.

For six months, since just before his wife's accident, he had been trying to find it again. Just like Mary's memories, he was rebuilding.

The men around the table grew restless as the hours ticked by. Charles could almost set his watch by them. There was a distinct moment when their minds had left the office and were already headed back home. All but one of them.

He ended the meeting and watched the ginger-haired man stay behind. He was moving through a different space than the rest. Everyone else knew what was behind them and what was ahead. They went from moment to moment without thinking. This man couldn't do that. His moments weren't his own anymore. They'd been taken and carried away. He moved like he was trying to stay in the last one that he recognized, waiting for the rest to lay out in front of him again.

Charles wondered how long it would take for him to accept they never would.

The man finished tucking his papers into his briefcase and gave a single nod toward Charles before starting for the door. Charles stepped up beside him.

"How are you doing, Helmsworth?" he asked. "Getting along alright?"

"As well as can be expected, I suppose," the younger man told him.

Charles followed him out of the conference room and walked alongside him, out of the office building.

"Like I told you, she's just being a woman. They get silly sometimes."

Helmsworth shook his head.

"Not Liza. She's never been that way. This isn't like her."

Charles paused next to his car and reached out his hand toward the other man.

"Let me know if there's anything I can do for you, Nick."

A flicker of emotion passed over Helmsworth's eyes, darkening the green just slightly.

"And your wife?" he asked. "How is she?"

"Showing progress every day," Charles said with a grateful sigh. "She's had a few setbacks, of course. The doctors prepared us for that. But we're choosing to focus on the ways she's getting better. We were looking at pictures of us over lunch, and I think she almost remembered."

"I'm glad to hear it."

"Have a good evening, Helmsworth. You know how to reach me if you need anything."

"Thank you. I'll see you tomorrow."

Charles ducked into the driver's seat and waited for his hands to warm the leather on his steering wheel before heading back home, glad to know Mary would be there waiting for him.

———

LB PROJECT – PG. 25

"BEHIND BLUE EYES": INT. LARGE, DINGY BATHROOM

A shower is audible in the background. A woman humming/singing quietly to herself. Steam covers the mirror. Just before it completely conceals the glass, the reflection of a DARK FIGURE appears in the corner.

INDISTINCT VOICE: (WHISPERS)

"Violet."

A hand wearing a black glove touches the glass and glides down. Words appear in the steam on the mirror. The dark figure steps away, revealing the message:

You can't leave yet

CHAPTER FOUR

NICK

When he wasn't listening, Nick Helmsworth called him 'The Boss'. Or sometimes just 'Boss'. When he was listening, Nick didn't call him anything. At least, not when he didn't have to. It's not that he disliked The Boss. It would be difficult to really dislike someone as overwhelmingly inoffensive as him. That's really the only way Nick could think of to fully encapsulate Boss. The name was almost a joke. He was in charge of the company and kept himself at the top of the hierarchy for all projects, but there was nothing aggressive or demanding about him.

At least, not usually. Nick had seen him riled up before. But only when it came to this particular project. It was all The Boss talked about. He had for more than two years now. What had started as an idea had become an obsession, eclipsing everything else. The only time they worked on anything else was when their schedule came to a grinding halt this summer.

That happens when someone dies.

Instead, Nick called him The Boss, because it kept him right in the position he wanted him in. If Nick used his last name, it fed into the power division and fracturing of the team. If Nick used his first name, it was too casual. So, it was Boss.

It already seemed like The Boss was angling for a friendship with Nick, acting like they were buddies who knew each other well enough to delve into the private realities of their marriages. He didn't dislike Boss, but they'd never tipped back a couple of beers and waxed poetic about what they were going through with their wives. Even after as much time as they had spent together, that sort of camaraderie had never existed between them. But if there was ever going to be an appropriate time to change that, Nick supposed this was it.

He'd been the first at the office to notice how uncharacteristically disheveled Boss looked that morning when he came into work. Nick had seen the dry reddish drops on the cuff of his sleeve and asked about them. He'd been the one to listen to the harrowing story of The Boss's wife and her accident, the sleepless night that followed, and the hazy morning getting dressed in un-ironed clothes and the shirt he'd been wearing when he stood beside her in the hospital.

Nick had gone home that night to hug his wife tight. At least he would have if he hadn't walked into a dark, empty house, and remembered it had been a week since she walked out. He couldn't hold Liza to him and breathe her in. He couldn't talk to her over dinner and shake the images from his mind. He couldn't tuck close into bed beside her and let her warm, bare skin reassure him.

All he could do was reread the note she left behind. Nick hadn't moved it from the place where he found it on the table in the foyer. The small silver bowl there was supposed to hold his keys. Now it held the piece of paper with his name emblazoned across the top and her sparse goodbye filling less than half of the empty space. There it all was. Liza condensing three years of marriage into half a piece of stationery, and nothing but her name in the empty space beneath.

That was in the blazing, suffocating heat of the summer. The temperature and humidity had crept up through June, egged on by the growing pressure at work. The Boss's project had collapsed, police and the papers were breathing down their necks, and Nick's climb up the ladder at the company had become even more precarious. Somewhere in there, he'd lost sight of Liza. He hadn't realized it. It was never his intention. Wherever he went, he thought of her. He squirreled away funny moments in his mind so he could share them with her later. He readily showed off her picture and talked about the life they were building together. Not newlyweds anymore. But not yet fully settled into the rhythm of their marriage.

Liza was always on his mind, whether she knew it or not. Apparently not.

Neglected. Ignored. Lonely.

Those were words Nick had heard from wives before, but not Liza. He never thought he'd hear them from her. But the note went on. In a handful of lines, she had dismantled their relationship and all he thought they'd shared. She resented having to work. She wanted a family. She hated the tiny house he'd presented to her after they got married.

Each word chipped away at Nick until he no longer knew what he was supposed to think. This wasn't the marriage he remembered. But maybe that was the problem. He lived so much in his own vision of the life they shared that it had never occurred to him that Liza might not be walking along beside him.

That was six months ago, and he was still alone. And The Boss insisted on checking on him with increasing frequency. It made sense. Christmas was days away, and there wasn't a single place Nick could go that didn't force on him reminders of what he should have and had lost. Every storefront, every advertisement, every song on the radio underscored Nick's emptiness.

But Boss made him feel worse. It wasn't like Nick could pretend this wasn't happening. Everyone at the office knew what was going on and had ever since he came in feeling drained of every drop of life. Some had offered the type of encouraging words you're supposed to give a friend going through something like this. They'd clapped him on the back and told him to keep his chin up. A few offered those cold beers and understanding, commiserating ears. But then they let it go. Conversations became gestures, became knowing looks, became pretending it wasn't happening because it was easier for everyone.

Except for Boss. He never stopped asking. It made Nick feel guilty that he'd give that much thought when he was dealing with plenty of his own with his wife's injuries. At the same time, Nick sometimes wondered if that's why The Boss asked him. He could stop worrying about his own troubles for a minute and remind himself that when he got home, at least he'd get to hold his wife. She may be gradually piecing the years of their marriage back together in her mind, but at least they weren't written across cream-colored stationery in blue pen and sitting at the bottom of a silver key-bowl.

Nick forced himself to stop thinking about Liza and let his brain drift back to work. Traffic was terrible with rush-hour commuters and holiday shoppers. He knew the trip home would move like the grey snow sludge moving down the gutters, and thinking about work meant he didn't have to torture himself thinking about Liza.

The first in-person hiring round had gone well that day. A crowd of women showed up in the lobby of the office, a sea of pencil skirts and leather gloves that assured they'd read the instructions carefully. The two who showed up in slacks were quickly escorted away. That would never do for The Boss. People got one chance to follow instructions and do things the way he wanted them. Not following them wasn't just a disappointment in that moment. It was a sign of a character flaw, and he had little patience for that when it came to his company.

With only four women to push through the rest of the process, there was actually a chance of selecting the right one before they broke for the holidays. That would be a weight off Nick's shoulders. Ever since Vanessa got spooked and walked off set, refusing to continue with the project, the need to replace her had been hanging on him. Technically, it wasn't meant to be his responsibility. There were other members of the team who were supposed to handle things like that. But Nick was determined to advance through the ranks and be recognized for as much as he put into his career. He didn't want to be on the outskirts forever. So, he took an active role in the tedious task.

A task that kept him at the office late. That took up many of his conversations with everyone who would listen.

She left just before Liza did. Just before the accident. Just before the project was put on an indefinite delay.

Then suddenly, none of the work mattered. Everything was being reimagined, and it didn't really matter that no one had heard from Vanessa and Nick hadn't found a replacement for her because the character was different. But no one knew how. The story was still being told, and until it was fully out of Boss's mind, they couldn't move forward.

Outside of Boss's thoughts, the LB Project lay dormant for weeks. They waded through red tape and made concessions just to salvage what they could. Other smaller projects grew, but it was always in the back of the team's awareness that any second, they'd be right back where they had been. Immersed in a story that edged too close to reality while still being impossibly far from the truth. An unexplainable mix of loyalty and morbid curiosity kept the team there.

They were all ready for it to be over.

CHAPTER FIVE

MARY

I finally have the living room decorated except for the tree. It looks even emptier now that the mantle is glistening with silver picture frames and bells tucked in among greenery, and each place where the windows should be has a wreath. These windows are different from the one in the kitchen. Right after the accident, when roaming through my own home felt like discovering each room and the details inside them for the first time, I asked Charles about them. He was as tender and supportive as he could be. He tried so hard to understand what I was going through. But how do you explain to someone what it's like to open your eyes, not remembering when you closed them? To wake up in a life you know is yours, but feels as strange and uncomfortable as wearing someone else's clothes?

It made my mouth tingle and ache to call him Charles in those first weeks. It was like my lips didn't know how to form the sound, and my throat tried to hold it back. I forced it through because I knew I had to. Eventually, it would feel right. Eventually, I would know him again. I would know the man who was so understanding of the crippling fears that define me that he replaced most of the windows in our home with rippling glass. Instead of smooth sheets like water that let you easily look through and see the world beyond the walls, these panes protect me. They let in just enough light to bolster the bulbs in the twin brass lamps sitting on end tables on either side of the couch. But the world beyond it is hazy and uncertain.

I can't be afraid of what I can't see. At least that's what Charles tells me. But the kitchen window, a large expanse that takes up the entire space above the sink, is different. The only one on this side of the house, it didn't get the wavy glass to give me light on my face when I wash the dishes.

"This is the window that bothered you the most when we first moved in," he told me, when I touched my fingertips to the piece of wood set into place in front of the window.

"Why?" I asked. "I don't understand why this window would be any different than any of the others in the house."

"It looks out over a lake," Charles told me. "It's just a small lake, a pond really. For many of the families who live in this neighborhood, it's one of the most appealing features. They moved here with images of summer picnics and evening walks. But for you... I can still see the look on your face when I brought you into this kitchen, and you saw that window. You looked out at the water beyond, and the neighbors gathered there, and you were so afraid."

"What was I afraid of?"

It felt so odd asking questions like that. It still does. Every day when I have to ask him something about me, to try to discover myself in his mind, I feel out of touch.

"When you were just a little girl, you almost drowned at a summer picnic with your family. Your parents were busy with your brother, and you wandered to the edge of a lake without anyone noticing you were there."

He hesitated then. The look in his eyes told me he didn't want to continue. The rest of the story was too much for me, and he didn't want to put it in my mind if I'd finally been freed from it. At the same time, he didn't want to have to think about it, either. But I insisted. Him holding on to pieces of me I'd lost was unfair and stood directly in the way of me knowing myself again. I knew he wanted me back as much as I wanted myself. In those earliest days and weeks, I wasn't

even his wife. Everything about me he'd fallen in love wi
and he had to carry on with the hope I still existed some
within myself.

Those little bits and pieces became currency. He gives
and in return, I use them to close the distance between m
who I am now. I prepare his favorite meals and keep t.
Charles tells me stories of when we were courting and deta
the family who lives too far away to have come to see me
accident. I wear the dresses he likes and dance with him to t
at night. Charles sings to me in his smooth, warm voice and r
me of all the other times I've heard these songs.

But the story of the kitchen window had a higher co
wouldn't offer it to me easily. I spent days cajoling it out of
trying to convince him those details were meant to be shared wit.
They were already there, somewhere. Everything that happened t
before the accident was there. It was just locked behind the walls
brain built that day. The doctors had already told us it was possibl
reclaim those years of my life. Sharing stories and reminding me
even the smallest details could make my memories break loose aga.
This could be the one. That story could be what I needed to make t
walls come down and be who I was before.

It finally worked.

Sometimes I wish it hadn't.

"That day, when you were at the lake with your family, it was very
crowded. You walked to the edge of the water just to put your toes in.
Your mother told me you always loved the water, but she never
wanted to let you in too far because she was afraid you would get
hurt. She always kept you close and made sure someone was with you
if you wanted to go in. That day they didn't pay attention when you
asked to go play in the water, and so you went on your own. You had
waded out a few feet when an animal in the water frightened a crowd
of swimmers. They ran back up onto the beach, not noticing you were
there. It forced you down into the water, and several people stepped
on you. You were pushed out into the lake and dragged down by the
animal."

"What kind of animal?"

"They never found out. When your family noticed you were missing and saw the thrashing in the water, your father went in after you. He didn't see the animal, but he said it could only be a very large fish or maybe an alligator. When he finally brought you to the surface, you had been bitten severely and were barely alive. You spent several weeks in the hospital recovering. Though your body recovered, your mind never truly did. That was when your agoraphobia started. You didn't want to leave the house. You didn't trust groups."

"How did we meet?"

My heart pounded harder with every one of his words. I kept my eyes locked on my husband, waiting for the movement of his lips and the flicker of his eyes to match something in my mind.

"Your parents insisted you would get better. They brought you out of the house as much as possible and encouraged you to do as many things as you could. We met when our families picnicked in the same place."

I nodded, trying to taste the summer-warm watermelon or feel the blanket beneath me when I looked into his eyes for the first time.

"You sealed the kitchen window because of the lake? Because I didn't like to see the people?"

Charles drew in a breath. It was one of the first things I'd learned about him. He took deep breaths to fill in space he didn't want to fill with words. It's like he thought if he could take enough time to draw it in that I'd forget what I'd asked him. Maybe he thought he was drawing the thoughts out of me and locking them into himself to hold with all the other fragments of me. It didn't deter me. I wanted to know. I needed to.

"No," he finally told me, resigned that I wasn't going to leave it alone. "When we first moved into this house, the kitchen window was like the rest of them. I had the glass replaced just like your father had in your room at home. You said it made you more comfortable. It stayed that way until six months ago."

"Six months ago?"

It twisted my already muddled mind.

"The summer has always been the favorite time for families to go to the lake. It was challenging for you, but you'd been getting stronger and were determined to get past your fear. We haven't had any children yet, and you wanted to get through these difficulties before you became a mother. I was so proud of you." His eyes got misty. "Every day you'd stand at the window and watch as much as you could and listen to the sound of the families for as long as you could. In the two weeks before, you'd been able to stand there for an hour. Then one afternoon, you heard screaming. You called to me. I ran in as fast as I could, but it was too late."

Bright white light flashed behind my eyes and the back of my throat burned with the remembered smell of anesthetic and medication.

"The accident."

I thought I said it out loud, but I realized it came from between my lips as a whisper barely louder than a breath.

Charles nodded.

"A gang of teenagers had come to the lake for some mischief. They frightened away the children and were wreaking havoc. You heard them, but you didn't see the rock they threw. It broke through the glass and hit your head. When I came home from being with you in the hospital, I couldn't bear to look at it or to repair the broken glass. I just sealed it up."

I remember the way those words felt sinking into me and moving through me like boiling water. They coiled in my stomach and burrowed in the back of my mind. They made the tiny hairs along the back of my neck stand up and the palms of my hands sweat.

It wasn't out of fear or trauma. Not a single word of the story sounded familiar.

They still don't, even now, as I walk into the kitchen and sit at the pink Formica table in front of a stack of Christmas cards. The list of recipients Charles gave me is a scatter of letters and numbers without meaning. I see no faces in the names, no images of homes, or rooms or front walkways in the addresses. But I carefully copy each to the front of an envelope and select a card from the stack. The paper feels as thick and dry as the thoughts I'm scouring for anything that's spontaneous and tangible. I unfold the crease and write inside like I know who will read them, like they will be able to see my face and sense my sincerity when they look at the words.

CHRISTMAS 1955

Jim and Sally,
    Wishing you and yours a Merry Christmas and Happy New Year.
    Charles and Mary

CHRISTMAS 1955

Valerie,
    Season's Greetings. Have a joyous holiday.
    Charles and Mary

CHRISTMAS 1955

David and family,
    May the warmth of the season be with you during the holidays and the new year bring you...

My pen stops. Black ink pools at the metal tip and filters out through the fibers of the paper like the spindly legs of an insect. What do I want the new year to bring them? I don't know what they might need, or what this year lacked for them. I don't even know what 'family' means. A husband, wife, and children? A single father? Several generations under one roof?

...WHAT YOU HOPE FOR.

Charles and Mary

. . .

I reach for another card, and an image flashes in front of my eyes. A surge of emotion fills me, and the room suddenly feels empty. It shouldn't just be me here. I shouldn't be sitting at this table by myself filling out these cards. There's someone missing.

Squeezing my eyes closed, I concentrate for a few seconds only on the way my breath feels coming in and out of my body and wait for the tiny pinpricks of colored light to stop bursting behind my eyes. Then I focus on the feeling, on the image I'd imagined only for a brief second. I try to bring it back so I can solidify it and know what's there.

A woman sitting across from me. Laughing, her hair bouncing over her shoulders as she tosses her head back and gives in. A pink sweater with sparkling sequins in the form of snowflakes in a curve from her shoulders down over her chest. Her bright eyes glitter when she looks at me, blue like ice, but holding all the warmth I should feel when writing these cards. A narrow silver band on one finger stands out against the slight golden tint of her skin when she reaches for another card to write.

I blink, and she's gone. I close my eyes tightly and hope the bright bursts of color will bring her back. They don't.

I'm left with nothing but Nat King Cole's voice leaving a trail along my skin and cool water on my fingertips as I touch a stamp to the sponge and put it in place.

CHAPTER SIX

LB PROJECT – PG. 67

"Behind Blue Eyes"

OPEN FIELD, TALL GRASS, A FEW WEEDS AND WILD-FLOWERS – TWILIGHT

VIOLET walks into view. She appears determined, like she knows exactly where she is going and what she's doing. She pauses for a few seconds, looking around, then continues through the field.

VIOLET: (V.O.)

People never really forget. The memories are there; they just can't find them.
But no matter what's lost, if you look long enough, you'll find it.

Camera sweeps down to VIOLET's hand. She's holding something blue, but the dim light makes it hard to identify. POV changes to show what VIOLET is seeing. It's getting darker, and the grass fades into the blackness ahead. The outline of trees is visible against the dark blue sky.

FEMALE VOICE: (WHISPERED)

"I'm still here. Still waiting."

————

Charles

The house smelled like chicken and popcorn when Charles stepped through the second front door that night. Outside, the light had faded to almost nothing, and the rosebushes looked skeletal against the white fence behind them. He remembered them in the spring when the flowers looked brighter, and the longer stretches of light warmed the manicured mulch beneath them. They looked sparser than he thought they would. Next year he would fill in with more bushes. White and light pink blooms. By then, Mary might be ready to enjoy them.

But not until after the new bushes went in.

"Darling?" he called out, remembering how much he startled her when he came home for lunch. "Where are you?"

"In the living room," Mary answered.

He hung his coat and hat and brought his briefcase down the hallway to this study. Tucking it away next to his desk, he locked the door behind him and went to greet his wife. She looked up from where she was perched on the couch beside a large bowl of popcorn. Another bowl on the other side of her brimmed with cranberries. The needle in her hand glinted in the flashing light coming from the television, where a cartoon holiday special filled the room with music. He knew she didn't care what was happening in the show. She just wanted the sound.

"Isn't this a lovely picture," he said as he paused in the doorway. She looked up at him and gave a modest smile. "It could be a Christmas card."

He sat down beside her and touched his lips to her cheek. She leaned slightly into the kiss. He gave her another, and she turned her mouth, so he caught the corner of her lips. One day he'd be greeted with a drink missing one sip and the taste of olives on her lips like before. The perfect, taste-tested drink. The perfect kiss for him to taste. It would come back. Maybe after she saw the roses. He could wait. He already had.

Mary held up the strand of popcorn and cranberries she had created.

"Almost finished," she said. "We can add it to the tree."

Charles smiled wider.

"Just the touch it needs."

Her long fingers slipped another piece of popcorn into place, then nestled a plump red berry against it. She looked up at him.

"I wrote the cards," she said.

"Good. I'll take them with me and put them in the mail tomorrow. They should arrive just in time for Christmas."

Mary nodded.

"While I was writing them, I had another vision."

His face dropped, and worry clenched his stomach.

"What happened, Darling? Are you alright?"

He moved closer to her across the cushions, but she didn't tremble or flinch.

"I'm fine. It wasn't frightening. It was… a woman."

"A woman?"

"It was like I could see her sitting at the table with me. It… it felt like she should be there writing the Christmas cards with me."

"Who was it?" Charles asked.

Mary shook her head, and some of the tightness loosened in his throat.

"I don't know," she admitted. "She seemed so familiar, but I couldn't place her." Her shoulders dropped with a heavy sigh. "I wanted so much for it to be a memory."

"What did she look like?"

"Pretty. Thick blonde hair. She was wearing a pink sweater with snowflakes."

Charles smiled.

"That's your sister," he said. "Vivian."

"My sister?" Mary asked.

Charles nodded enthusiastically.

"Yes. She is older than you, and the two of you used to love preparing for Christmas together." He leaned in for a kiss against her temple and then stood. "It's wonderful that you remember her."

"But I didn't. I could just see her in my mind."

"That's a start. Even the littlest glimpses are a step in the right direction. You'll have to be sure to tell the doctor."

"The doctor?" she asked.

"I'm sorry, Darling. I forgot to mention it to you. There is a doctor who came highly recommended by the hospital. He specializes in people going through memory loss and struggling with your... challenges. I got in touch with him, and he is sympathetic to your situation. He is willing to come to the house to see you for now."

"For now?"

"Of course. Soon, he'll help you get to the point where you can go to see him."

Mary's eyes moved toward the wavy glass of the living room window. Her hands still gripped the popcorn and cranberries as they settled into her lap.

"Do you really think that will happen?" she asked.

"I do. He will help you. And I will be right here with you. Now, come on. Supper smells so good I feel like I haven't eaten in a week."

Mary didn't return his chuckle, but her emerald eyes moved to him.

"You never mentioned a sister."

Charles tilted his head at her.

"What do you mean?"

"My sister, Vivian. You've never mentioned her before when you talked about my family."

"I haven't?"

She shook her head.

"No. You've talked about my parents and brothers, but never a sister."

Tension shortened the muscles that ran along his spine, and his mind went to the trunk in the attic. There were pictures in it. There had to be. He smiled so she wouldn't see the search in his eyes.

"Silly me. I must not have told you any stories about her. It has been several years since you've seen her, after all."

"Why?"

"She's married to a military man, and they moved out to California. With his injuries from the war, it's not easy for him to travel. And, of course, such a journey has not been an option for you."

Mary's always-questioning eyes slid over his mouth for a few seconds, waiting to gather any more words that might form there. When they didn't, she stood up and walked past him into the kitchen.

"There are glazed carrots to go with the chicken," she said.

The faint dusting of flour over the top of the recipe box beside the stove captured the fingerprints on the smooth surface.

CHAPTER SEVEN

NICK

The container of macaroni and cheese he took out of the freezer for dinner was still cold in the middle when Nick sat down in front of the television to eat it. He didn't know how to reheat it and didn't care enough to get up and try again when the cold-congealed sauce hit his tongue. It's not like he tasted it. The only reason he was eating at all was to settle the sick feeling in his stomach and stop the shaking from long stretches without bothering to swallow anything. Chewing through the yellow-coated elbows also kept his mouth occupied, so he didn't call out for Liza.

Whatever was playing out on the television screen and didn't sink into his mind flashed brighter on his face because of the darkness in the rest of the room. He washed down each bite with a swig of rum. It should have found its way into the bottom of a bowl of eggnog by this point in the season, but he didn't bother. The sugar-and-spice laced cream would just muddle the transit for each burning sip.

Only three more days of work until the company closed down for the holidays. It wouldn't open again until after the new year. Nick felt certain he was the only one among his coworkers who was dreading those three days going by and the time off starting. At least work gave him eight solid hours away from the house every day. Sometimes more, when there was something to distract him even more. It minimized the time he spent at the house, thinking about Liza and how they should be celebrating together.

A stack of mail had grown on the sideboard and toppled over, so it spread across the polished wood in a spill of red, green, and gold studding the usual stream of white envelopes. They were greeting cards he didn't intend to open, and invitations to parties he wouldn't attend. He didn't want to look at the addresses. The ones made out only to him were as bad as the ones that still listed Liza. One isolated him as a separate entity from her. One underscored that she wasn't there.

Sometimes he hazarded a glance through the mail he brought in each day. Looking only at the return addresses, he had his eye out for Liza's handwriting. It was distinctive and so familiar to him Nick probably could have identified it by a single letter. But it hadn't shown up. Not in six months. It wouldn't have made much sense if it had, but he wouldn't let himself think that. There was still a part of him that hadn't yet withered and faded. It was doing more than going through the motions, and it was that part of him that kept him looking for a note from her.

Even though she had been the one to walk away

Even though she had specifically instructed him not to try to contact her.

That hadn't stopped him. He didn't care who told him not to; he wasn't going to stand by and let Liza walk out of his life without at least trying to go after her. He kept trying. Sometimes it was so he could beg her to come back home. Sometimes it was so he could sweep her into his arms and bring her home even if she argued. Sometimes it was so he could scream and shout at her for putting him through this. Sometimes it was just so he could ask why.

No matter what the reason, it hadn't worked. He called every number he could think to dial and left as many messages as he could, but she never picked up or called him back. He went to every place in town he thought she might go and searched for her, but she was never there. Liza had always been a determined woman, and this time she was determined to be gone.

Nick sat on the couch and stared at the television until long after he scraped the last of the cheese sauce from his bowl. The night had hit its peak and would soon tip over into the downward slide to morning. He knew he needed to stretch out across his bed and close his eyes. Not sleep. He wasn't sure he'd actually slept since summer. Instead, he'd lie like that and wait. On the bad nights, stories played out on the backs of his eyelids, and he rolled out of tangled, sweaty sheets in the morning to stare out of the window and let the sun burn the images away. On the good nights, his body shut down and went into unmoving, unthinking blackness until he came to, stiff, aching, and still exhausted. It wasn't sleeping. It was surviving.

That was one of the good nights. He didn't have to lie there thinking there was a time when he believed Liza would never have just walked away, that she would never want to not talk. Liza talked more than any person he had ever known, even when no one seemed to be listening. One time, two years ago, before that summer, before the overtime, before Christmas, he asked her why. She walked around the house talking like there was always someone with her, and many times he lost the ends, or even the beginnings, of conversations to other rooms. She told him she liked to imagine the words were still there waiting to be heard.

He envisioned them like encapsulated droplets, hanging around in the air throughout the house, waiting for him to walk through them. In the days after she first left, he wandered through the rooms of their tiny home, covering every inch of the pale beige carpet and speckled tile floor with his footsteps. Maybe if he could find some of those words, it would tell him what happened and why she left so suddenly.

When his eyes opened, it was morning. Not the bright type of morning that smelled like rain and pancakes and sounded like birds. A cold, grey morning that seemed to be trying to recycle the moonlight and make it last through the entire day. Those were the kinds of mornings that were disorienting when sleep didn't give any reprieve from exhaustion. Nick might have lain there for hours, already late to work. His eyes could have only been closed for long enough for the very darkest part of the night to end. Or it could have been only a few, fleeting seconds. He couldn't even tell.

The clock told him it was his usual wakeup time. Just enough morning ahead of him to take a shower, swallow down black coffee and toast, and drive to the office. Outside, the air bit into him. It was colder than it had been in the last few weeks. The dampness in the air made the cold cling and gave it time to sink deeper into his skin. The heater had just started to kick in and take away the chill by the time Nick pulled into the office parking lot. There were only a few other cars there. That's how he liked it. Arriving early gave him the advantage of gauging everyone else as they got to work.

He could tell which ones were in a good mood.

Which ones had an axe to grind.

Which were going straight for the coffee.

Which had a flask in their inside pocket.

Which would sit in the back corners and slide by the best they could.

Which would stomp on the heads of anyone in their way to get where they wanted to go.

That morning, he used the time to sit in the car with the heater pumping out stinging breath on his face and thawing his toes. He stared through the windshield without really seeing anything. The sky was layers of gray. Everything silhouetted against it looked dead and empty. He didn't know how long he sat there until the gray at the corner of his eye blurred away to baby blue.

The Boss had arrived. That was another reason Nick usually arrived at work early. He got there before everyone else, so he didn't have to walk across the parking lot with Boss. So he didn't have to share the elevator. So he didn't have to start his day with the sympathetic looks. He never said it. He never said anything that wasn't supportive and compassionate, but his eyes said something different. Behind them was the unspoken commentary.

"My wife might not remember, but at least she's still here."

CHAPTER EIGHT

MARY

I should know him. Even if my mind doesn't completely remember. Even if most of my thoughts and memories are still locked away somewhere I can't yet reach, I should know him. My body should remember his touch. My skin should know his skin. I should know his taste and the smell of his sweat. He should have left an imprint on me that makes my body remember him, ache for him, feel complete with him.

But I don't. I wake up in the morning cold, but I don't move across the mattress toward his warmth just inches from mine. The bed is so small, and I know I shouldn't, but I find myself clenching my body into the smallest space possible rather than letting my skin meet his again. He doesn't repulse me. I don't hate him. I just don't know him. Our bodies don't move together. Our hands don't reach for one another at the same time. When his weight pushes me down into the mattress, I don't feel enveloped and protected. I just can't breathe.

This isn't how I should feel. I know that, and the guilt gets deeper every morning when there's no change. I cover it with a perfectly pressed dress and a swipe of black eyeliner. I bury it deep in pancake batter and fresh coffee. Charles won't know. He can't know. I won't stop trying to make it different one morning.

The doctor Charles arranged to talk to me is coming this afternoon. Somehow, that makes the morning seem longer and shorter at the same time. Knowing he's coming makes me feel strangely anxious. Even if I can't see what's just below my own surface, something tells me I have to protect it. Look perfect. Keep a perfect home. Be a perfect hostess.

But I'm not a hostess. He's not coming here to be entertained or taste the sugar cookies baking in the oven. I'm a patient, and he's coming to try to help me. But that doesn't stop the minutes from ticking past and the worry from creeping up as it feels like I don't have enough time to get ready before he arrives.

And yet, there's still hours in front of me, and too much time to fill with only tidying. With less than two weeks until Christmas and only days until the party, the list of things I need to get done is long. Just thinking about the party makes me nervous, but I throw myself into the next task, so I don't have to think too much about it. Focusing in close to just one thing means I don't have to think about the larger picture. I can make a menu without thinking about the people coming to eat from it. I can wrap presents without thinking about the pressure of Christmas morning.

That's what I'm doing now as I wait for the seconds to slip into minutes to melt into hours until the doctor comes. Because then he will leave. I just want to get through the appointment. The boxes sitting beside me as I kneel in front of the coffee table help to distract me. I hope Charles doesn't realize I chose his gifts completely at random. When the catalogs arrived, I flipped through them and filled the order card with the first things that stood out to me. Of course, Charles handled the payment. He didn't mention the amount, so I suppose I didn't choose too much.

I don't want to open all the boxes at once and risk spoiling the surprise if Charles comes home unexpectedly, so I work through one at a time. The shirt in front of me is crisp and fresh, each pleat exactly in its place. Carefully snipping away the price tag, I fold the red and black plaid and settle it into the tissue paper in a shirt box. Little elves playing in the snow printed on the lid of the box make it pretty enough to just tuck under the tree, but I arrange it in the center of a piece of wrapping paper anyway.

When I smooth the final piece of tape onto the package and add a curling bow on top, I gather up the two other boxes I've wrapped so I can find a place to hide them. There isn't space beneath the couch, and that would make vacuuming far more difficult. Charles goes into the liquor cabinet too often not to notice gifts tucked away there.

I glance behind the television into the space I've never paid much attention to. The set is close to the wall, so there is very little space, and what is there is crowded with wires and cables, small strange metal boxes and a blinking light that puts me on edge. I don't know why, but that light bothers me.

Pretending I haven't seen it, I carry the boxes out of the living room and through the rest of the house. First into the kitchen. Charles doesn't go into the cabinets or pantry often, but there is little space that won't ruin my careful organization. Besides, I wouldn't want a bottle of oil or jar of something to break and ruin the gifts. I go into the hallway and pause beside the door to Charles's study. It's locked. I know it is. It always is. Our bedroom was next, but even our closet would be too obvious. I'd already seen the cheerful red paper of a small stack of gifts tucked into the back corner of the top shelf and hastily covered with a hat. Charles had claimed that as his hiding space already and it wouldn't do any good to try to trick him by hiding his gifts there, too.

That means there is only one room left. The closed door at the end of the hallway. Charles insists on calling it the nursery. This, he always tells me, is where our children will sleep. His eyes get misty and his voice hopeful when he talks about that. A baby is what would complete us. He wants us to be a true family. After years of marriage, we've had the time to enjoy just being together, and it's time to raise our own little ones.

The thought makes the back of my neck tingle and the muscles along my back ache.

He calls it the nursery, but that's not what it is. Whatever my husband envisions for the future, for now, the room is a guest bedroom scattered with a few items Charles says are supposed to go into the attic but never seem to have found their way there. I slip inside and glance around. There isn't often cause for me to come in here. We haven't had overnight guests, and the boxes stored in here mostly belong to Charles from when he was younger. They're all marked with his name and stacked against the wall. Sometimes curiosity gets to me, but I haven't let it take over yet. The only other times I need to come in here are for twice-monthly cleaning. With no one else here, the brush of the vacuum and sweep of the dust cloth only takes a few minutes.

I'm always grateful for that. This room isn't my favorite part of the house. There's really no reason why. It's neatly decorated and taste-fully kept. The rippled glass of the windows looks welcoming, framed in the blue and white floral curtains that are always pulled back. But something in the air changes when I walk into this space. It feels like it's waiting. I take a step inside and get the feeling along my spine that I've just walked into a moment that is long over.

But it's the perfect hiding spot. I rush across the room and open the closet. It's empty except for a suit and evening gown pressed against the far end of the bar and an old hatbox sitting up on the shelf. The wrapped gifts fit into the other corner of the shelf perfectly. I'm starting to back out of the closet when the hatbox catches my eye. It must be mine, but I don't know what's inside.

Rising up on the balls of my feet, I reach for the hatbox. It's pushed back against the wall of the closet, putting it just out of reach. My fingertips touch the curved side, and I walk them across the smooth surface of the paper, easing it closer to me. Just as it inches to the edge and I'm almost able to grab it, I lose my balance. Toppling forward, I reach one hand ahead of me to break my fall. It hits the wall, and I feel something give beneath my fingertips. I find my footing again and pull my hand back, startled by the unexpected texture of the wall.

White wallpaper dotted with pale blue flowers is the perfect accompaniment to the curtains hanging at the window. It lines the walls of a closet that have been perfectly aligned to create a seamless accent to the rest of the room. Only now, it's not so perfect.

Just in front of me, a section of the wallpaper is dented down. Where it should be flush against the wall, it buckled in under my hand. Now a tiny tear forms along something hard. My fingertips trembling, I run them down along the hard rolled edge beneath the paper. I trace them along, feeling the rectangular shape and the dip inside. Just beneath the tear, another shape now pushes out against the paper. Running my fingers around the edge, I try to envision what it is. Metal. A rod nestled between hooks, with a small round knob hanging down.

A latch means something being held closed, locked so it won't open.

Wallpaper over it means someone wanting it to disappear.

I try to think of any time I've been in this closet. I know I have been. At some point, I opened that door and looked inside. The hatbox is familiar enough that I know the pattern along the paper, and I know the gown hanging behind this suit shimmers with champagne-colored sequins. But I never noticed anything strange about the wallpaper. It was just there. Always perfect, exactly the way it was supposed to be. There was no reason to question it.

Until now.

My fingers want to pull away at the paper. I want to force the tear open and see the door. And at the same time, I don't. Nothing can make this go away. Something has shifted. I can't pretend I don't see this. But I can also stop myself from going any farther. Taking a step back out of the closet doesn't feel right. The force of the room behind me and the waiting, anticipating feeling that hangs over it stops me. It holds me in place in the doorway, staring at the torn wallpaper.

Before I can even decide if I'll look any further, a bell chiming through the house stops me. My heart leaps up into my throat, and I can't force my breath out for a few seconds before I realize it's the doorbell. The doctor must have gotten here. I can't imagine how long I've been standing in the guest room, staring into the closet and wondering what might be behind a door someone – my husband – covered with wallpaper.

Smoothing my hair back into place, I close the closet door and rush out of the bedroom. I open the front door and see a tall, gray-haired man standing in the tunnel-like hallway between the house and the second front door. He smiles at me.

"Mrs. Whitman?"

I nod.

"Yes."

"My name is Dr. Baker. Your husband told me about the doors and hid a key for me outside. I hope that's alright with you."

I swallow deeply, forcing the feeling of the closet and the dip in the wallpaper down.

"Of course," I say. "Please, come in."

The doctor steps inside. I reach for his coat and hat. They don't feel cold against my hands, and I wonder how long he stood in the hallway before ringing the doorbell. My cheeks burn. I know the construction of the house is bizarre and like nothing he's ever seen. This man is the type who has seen far more than I ever have and has helped people in many ways. He's likely never seen something like this, and I feel like he's already forming thoughts about me.

He looks around and takes a subtle sniff. There's no coffee in the air. But there is the sweetness of sugar cookies. I usher him into the living room and rush to the kitchen to start the coffee. Coarse sugar falls like ice over the cookies, and I stack them high on a plate etched with a Christmas tree. Dr. Baker waits until I've settled the tray into place on the table in front of him, and then gestures to the chair where Charles sits to read the newspaper.

"Please," he says. "Sit."

There's something particularly disconcerting about being invited to sit down in your own living room. It immediately makes me feel like the doctor knows more about me than I realize. More about me than I do. I perch at the very edge of the seat cushion, crossing my ankles beneath the chair and smoothing my skirt down. The doctor takes his time pouring a cup of coffee and keeps his eyes trained on me as a long sip flows down his throat and readies him for our conversation.

Maybe he's trying to figure out something else about me. He's watching my reaction, but I don't know what it's supposed to tell him. Finally, he sets the half-empty mug on the table and takes a small notebook and pen from the pocket inside his suit jacket.

"May I call you Mary?" he asks.

"Yes," I tell him.

He jots something down.

"Tell me about yourself."

I almost laugh, but it feels inappropriate.

"I don't know what to tell you."

He gives me an empathetic smile.

"Charles tells me you've been having visions," he leads. "Why don't you tell me about that?"

"They come to me during the day," I start. "I never know when or what I'll be doing. It can be anything and they just happen."

"What just happens?" he asks.

"I'll see something, but I'm not really seeing it. It flashes in my mind and is almost real. Just not fully. Sometimes it's me running."

"Running from what?"

I shake my head.

"I don't know. I never know. There's something or someone chasing me, and I'm terrified. All I can think about is trying to get away."

"Do you?" he asks.

"The vision always stops." I shake my head. "I don't even know if I should be calling it a vision. That sounds so strange."

"What else would you call it?"

"I would hope it's a memory," I tell him.

His eyebrows raise questioningly.

"You hope you have a memory of running for your life from someone?"

The condescending tone in his voice is slick, and I wish he wasn't here.

"I hope I have a memory of anything," I insist.

His hand stops scribbling on his notebook, and gray eyes look into mine.

"What else? What else do you see?"

"A woman," I tell him. "It felt like she should be there while I was filling out Christmas cards to send. Charles told me I was remembering my sister, but..."

"But?"

"I still couldn't remember her. Charles had never mentioned a sister to me before, and it sounded so out of place when he said it. I just don't understand. If that was my sister and I knew her enough to remember her sitting with me while I sent Christmas cards, shouldn't I remember?"

"Do you remember your husband?"

The question clenches my heart and my stomach, and I feel my spine stretch and harden like steel.

"No," I finally whisper.

"Of everyone in your life, your husband is closest to you. He is closer than your parents or your siblings. He shares your life, is one flesh with you."

My face burns. My eyes drop to my lap, and I can see my legs shaking beneath my crinoline and skirt.

"Yes," I murmur.

"But it doesn't bother you that you don't remember him?"

My eyes snap up to his.

"Of course, it bothers me. Every day. I try as hard as I can to remember my life before the accident, to remember him. He has taken such good care of me and continues to love me every day. He hasn't faltered even once. I don't even want to tell him about my dreams or my visions because I feel like I'm burdening him. He's so busy and works so hard. He shouldn't have to deal with me being this way, too."

"What do you remember about your childhood?"

Everything inside me feels raw and unsteady from the bitterness that rolled out of me. His indifference and ability to smooth over it and move on only makes it worse. I don't want him here. I don't want to keep talking. But I know I have to. Charles has passed the currency of who I am and what is behind me on to this doctor. Of all of them who have worked with me, all the men in their white coats and concerned stares, maybe this will be the one who knows how to crack down the walls that hold me in.

"Nothing," I tell him.

"Nothing?"

He's expecting something. It's clear in his voice and the way he holds himself. It's clear in the tilt of the pen, with ink shivering on the piece of paper and waiting to form whatever he is recording. Just like I do with Charles, I offer him a little of what he wants. I repeat stories my husband has told me. I try to put myself into it and make the words sound like my own.

"How about your husband? Your marriage? Are there pictures you can show me?"

I take the silver frames from the mantle and offer them over, then pull an album from beneath the coffee table. Every page of this album has my fingerprints. Charles and I have gone over them what feels like a thousand times before. I tell the doctor the same things he told me. This is why we were recording. Our wedding. His cousins. The dog I had as a child.

"What do you feel when you look at these pictures and tell those stories?" he asks.

I draw in a breath and let it out slowly. Just like Charles.

"Like I'm trying to live someone else's life."

"When did you start feeling like that?"

"When I woke up."

CHAPTER NINE

LB PROJECT – PG. 80

"Behind Blue Eyes"

WATER. BRIGHT DAYLIGHT.

View is half-water, half-daylight. Camera moves down to full water, then back up to show sunlight. Sound of BENJAMIN breathing starts faint, almost covered by the sound of the water moving, then gets louder until it is audible. Sudden gasp as camera drops sharply into the water.

INDISTINCT VOICE: (WHISPERS)

"It had to be you."
VIOLET
(V.O.)
"It was always her."

FADE OUT.

————

Charles

Charles hated the way the small boutique smelled. It was a combination of spicy potpourri and the heavy perfume born by the woman who owned the shop. Some of the smell seeped out around the door, so he started breathing it in before he even stepped inside. But this is the only place he could find exactly what he needed. The only place that met his standards. Everything had to be perfect, and this was the only place where it was.

Bells jingled softly overhead when he opened the door. Charles resisted the urge to look up and see if they were silver, trotted out for the holiday season. Angela looked up from the glossy magazine spread open on the front counter. She gave him a smile that didn't quite reach her green eyes. Even from where he stood, he could see the red of her lipstick spreading into the fine lines and cracks around her mouth. Her contrast against the beautiful items that filled her shelves and hung on racks carefully arranged around the shop was a sharp imbalance.

"Back again, Mr. Whitman?" she asked.

It was her way of greeting him. Just another chip out of the image she could be. A reminder of why it was never her. It could have been. Years ago. Before Mary. Before anyone. It could have been Angela.

But lipstick in fine lines and dismissal in her greeting left her here.

"Good afternoon, Angela."

"Are you looking for something specific today?"

One hand flipped the magazine closed, and she moved around the counter toward him. Now that she walked toward him, she smiled like she wanted it to have been her. She'd never know it wouldn't be.

"I'm planning a holiday party. Mrs. Whitman will need a dress."

"Anything else?"

There was a note in her voice, one he'd heard before. It said she didn't want to hear him mention his wife. Out of sight, out of mind. She wanted his attention, even if he wasn't willing to give it to her. Probably because of it.

"Bring me your best holiday dresses, and I will look around for everything else."

She gave a terse nod and walked away. Charles waited until Angela had disappeared into the back room before he started browsing through the shop. He picked up a few items and turned them over in his hands before placing them back on the shelf. Others he placed on the counter. He might not find everything he had in mind, but there was still time. It took several minutes for Angela to return with a rack of dresses. She ran her hand along all of them to straighten them on their hangers, then turned to Charles.

"These just came in. They're different from the ones you saw the last time you were here." She reached for a bright blue sheath. "If she liked the one she wore last Christmas, this might be nice."

He looked at the dress and imagined Mary in it.

"I prefer that one," he said, pointing to an emerald green cocktail dress.

Angela looked at the dress with a hint of disdain but said nothing. She carried the dress over to the counter and added up everything he'd selected.

"Will I see you again before the holidays?" she asked, sweetness like her thick perfume now dripping from her voice.

"If there's anything else I need."

———

That evening, he carefully unpacked everything from the slim green-tinted paper bags in his workshop. Coming here would keep his work out of Mary's sight. He didn't want to ruin the surprise. A bright light above him and another lamp in the corner of the table, he spent hours painstakingly working on creating the perfect Christmas. With the party coming up soon, every detail mattered.

He spent as long as he could in the workshop before reluctantly pulling himself away. Mary would worry if he was gone too late. As it was, she was already in her nightgown when he walked into the house. She appeared at the end of the hallway, peering around the corner uncertainly.

"Charles?"

There was no sleep in her voice, so he kissed her. Held her close.

"I'm sorry I'm late, Darling. We're trying to set everything in place before the office closes for the holidays. You didn't have to wait up for me."

"I couldn't sleep," she said. "There's a bowl from supper waiting for you in the kitchen."

"Thank you. Will you heat it up for me?"

She nodded, and Charles headed for his study. When his briefcase was tucked away and the door locked, he walked toward the bedroom but paused in the middle of the hallway. Behind him, he could hear Mary in the kitchen, warming up whatever she'd cooked for him. He glanced back over his shoulder and then went into the bedroom to change clothes.

"How was your session with the doctor this afternoon?" he asked as she settled the bowl of chicken and dumplings in front of him.

Her hands curled around a cup of steaming tea as she sat across from him and nodded.

"He was very nice."

Charles took a bite of supper and gave Mary an encouraging nod.

"But?"

"I felt like he already knew about me and just wasn't telling me. Every time I said something, it was like he was testing me."

"He wasn't testing you, Darling. But he did know about you," Charles said.

"Why?"

"Because I told him, of course. When I contacted him and asked if he would come to help you, I thought it was important to make him understand the extent of the situation. He has worked with many patients before, but never my wife."

She smiled and glanced down, color touching her cheeks. That shyness was one of the reasons he stayed so devoted to her. It was sweet and frothy, delicate and innocent. Exactly what he wanted when he chose her.

"What does he know?"

"As much as I thought I needed to tell him. I told him about these nightmares of yours, and the images that are frightening you so much. He wanted to know how extensive your memory loss was after the accident and how much you had regained."

"He asked if I remember being a child," Mary said. "I don't."

"I know. But Dr. Baker reassured me that is very normal. Memory loss as profound as yours takes time to resolve. You're more likely to remember little bits from more recent years first, and then hopefully, your deeper memories will return."

Mary shifted uncomfortably.

"If you had already spoken to him and he knew all those things, why did he ask me?" she asked.

"He had heard my perspective, but he needed to hear it from you. He'll be coming by to work with you more often, and he needs to know how open you will be with him."

"Do I have something to hide?"

Charles didn't like the way the question settled into the bowl in front of him, and he pushed it away, dropping his spoon through the surface to dissipate it.

"You are doing something very brave, Mary. It isn't easy to talk about such personal things with a man who isn't your husband."

The delightful color crept into her hairline and down along the sides of her neck.

"And you are alright with it?" she asked.

Charles reached across the table and took her hands in his. They were warm from the tea and soft from the thick cream she rubbed into them every night. It smelled like roses.

"If it will bring you back to me, wholly and completely, I will be happy with whatever it takes." The faint shimmer of tears made her expression hazy, and he squeezed her hands. "Let's talk about something more exciting. Are you almost ready for the party?"

"What are you finishing up at work?" she asked.

His smile faltered, but he forced it to stay in place.

"Work?" he asked. "Why are you suddenly interested in my work?"

"You've been so late coming home," she said.

"Darling, you can't think there's someone else."

He wondered what images had been filling her mind when he was gone. Pink sweaters with snowflakes. Grass beneath her feet. The fear of water rising up over her eyes.

Mary shook her head.

"No. I only meant you have been working so hard and staying late so often. It must be interesting."

Charles brushed his fingertips along the curve of her face. With the layer of makeup gone for the night, her skin felt smooth and damp. His thumb traveled over to her lips and felt hot breath quicken from between them.

"It would be too intense for you," he murmured.

"It isn't real," she said.

The words made her lips move across his skin before she moved her face away.

"It was," he told her. "It happened a long time ago."

"What did?"

"Not tonight. I want only good dreams in your beautiful little head tonight."

CHAPTER TEN

NICK

The entire house sparkled.

If there was one thing Liza never quite got a hold of, it was subtlety in Christmas decorating. Every year she vowed to make it the year she acted like an adult and made the house beautiful for the holidays. By the beginning of November, she would have chosen a theme and started coming up with grand schemes for how it would flow seamlessly from room to room and make their home look elegant and sophisticated. By Thanksgiving, her excitement would translate to buying boxes of ornaments and decorations. Halfway through December, rolls of wrapping paper that matched the tree and harkened back to the details throughout the home would line up like little soldiers along the wall.

By the week before Christmas, she'd discover the box of childhood ornaments and decorations her grandmother passed down to her. Mice made from walnuts. Quilted hearts faded with age. Candy canes formed in clay by tiny hands that hadn't been tiny in many years. One by one, they'd appear on the tree, nestled in with the new ornaments. Then would come the favorites from the year before because she couldn't bear to not see them out again.

Christmas morning, they would open presents in a cacophony of festive touches.

The new year changed over with a promise. One day. One day, we'll decorate like adults.

November first, it started again.

But not that November. The first had come and gone with no new inspiration. No new magazine pages pinned to walls or ideas haphazardly sketched with no discernible skill on the backs of menus and shopping lists.

Nick had taken out all her boxes. He'd lined them up like little soldiers. He'd cut through every strip of tape and pulled out the ornaments and tinsel, candleholders, and snow globes. The only thing he left were the old boxes that had been opened dozens of times. He left her childhood where it was and instead filled their house with every whim she'd had since the fall they met.

That was the year everything was bright pink and silver.

Nick draped the final piece of tinsel over the bough of a Christmas tree he'd dragged out of the attic that morning and pieced back together like he was performing a resurrection ceremony. The glow from the multiple strands of lights, some white, some colored, reflected off the individual strands to make the entire tree shimmer.

It was all there. Every piece. Every year.

He didn't know if he was celebrating or mourning. Maybe neither. Probably both.

He was going through the motions of what he thought he was supposed to be doing, morbidly filling the long hours left empty when the office closed, and he couldn't show up to the parking lot to decipher his coworkers. The decorations taunted him but stayed silent. Not another song. Not another movie. Not another special about Christmas.

At least decorating kept the bitterness in his mind from forming into the shapes of the summer. He could bear the sugary idealism of decorating even if it sent tears down his cheeks. Those tears belonged to what should have been, not what already was. The summer shapes were too cruel. He didn't want to think about the days that led up to

Liza leaving. They weren't anything new. He'd gone over them a thousand times, repeated them over and over, trying to find a moment when he could have changed it.

In the handful of lines she left behind, Liza had only asked one thing of him. Not to contact her. To leave her alone and let her start living her life again. Nick couldn't honor it. He had for the first three days. But when the shock he first felt gave way to sadness and then to panic, he couldn't do it anymore. He had to find her. Even if she wouldn't come back right then, he needed to hear her voice and tell her he was still there.

It had been six months since he'd heard her voice. No matter how much he tried to reach out to her, he hadn't heard back. She had never answered the phone. She'd never written back. He looked and found no sign of her. It was obvious this hadn't been a choice she made quickly. Compulsion hadn't taken her away. Impulse let people disappear. It took a carefully drawn plan to keep them hidden.

Nick sat on the sofa and watched the lights shift and move. When he couldn't take it anymore, he stood and walked into the next room where the phone sat silent. He didn't know what time it was, but he picked it up anyway. He dialed number after number, listened to ring after ring after ring. Then emptiness. Another number. Another ring. Emptiness.

With every one, the worry faded, and the anger bubbled up. When the last ring fell silent, everything crashed. Nick barely registered walking down the hall and crossing the living room. He didn't feel the broken glass beneath his feet as the ornaments shattered on the floor. He didn't hear the smash of the decorations as he swept them off the mantle and toppled the bookshelf. Only his screams resonated through the house.

Sometimes there were words. Other times there was nothing but the guttural sound of everything inside him being torn out and cast on the floor among the broken glass and smashed ceramic.

He ripped everything from the branches of the tree, then pulled it apart into its pieces. Flimsy metal bent in his hands and cracked against the walls as he threw them. Finally, he sensed the stinging sensation roll up from his hands along his arms. Blood pooled on his palms and rose in tiny droplets along the inside of his forearms. It smeared across his skin and onto his clothes as he continued to thrash his way through the decorations.

When it was all destroyed, he collapsed. For the first time in six months, he really slept.

———

Nick stayed deeply asleep through the night and long into the morning. It wasn't the sound of his alarm clock that finally woke him, but the piercing ring of his phone. His eyes ached as his eyelids, dry and coarse like sandpaper, slid up. The ring made a backdrop of sound as first his sliced hands and then his pierced feet pressed into the ground to lift him to standing. Taking in the aftermath of what he had done, he made his way across the room and toward the phone.

"Hello?" he said.

His mouth was sour and sticky, and the word felt like the creak of his jaws pulling apart.

"Nick?"

The buzzing in his ears made it difficult to identify the voice.

"Hello?" he repeated, at a loss for anything else.

"Nick? Are you there? It's Matilda."

His mind went clear.

"Matilda? Where is she? Where is she?"

"Calm down. I can barely understand you. Have you been calling the house?"

He swallowed hard, trying to force enough moisture down his throat so he could speak.

"Yes. Where is she?"

"Who, Nick? Where is who?"

"Liza."

The other end of the line went silent for several long, painful seconds.

"What do you mean, where is Liza? Isn't she at home?"

"No. I thought she might have gone to you. I've been trying to get in touch with her, but every time I called, no one answered."

"Of course, no one answered. We haven't been home. Remember?"

Nick cringed. His stomach turned. Every ounce of fury and hatred he had been feeling sizzled and sank inward into himself. Matilda, his mother-in-law. Matilda, Liza's mother. Liza's mother who worked with her father on research projects that often took them away from their home on the other side of the world and any form of communication for months at a time. They left a week before Liza did. In the chaos, he had forgotten.

"You haven't heard from her?" Nick asked, this sick feeling getting worse.

"Not since we said goodbye before her father and I left. Just like always. Nick, what is going on?"

His head was spinning. How could he have forgotten his in-laws weren't in the country? All this time, he had imagined her there with them, let himself believe she was tucked away in her childhood bedroom, reconstructing her life like he had never been in it. It had been infuriating, heartbreaking, and reassuring all at the same time. If she was there, at least she was safe. Now...

"Liza left me."

He didn't say the words. Instead, they burst out of him like he was making a confession. The pause on the other end of the line was too long.

"She left you?" Matilda finally said. "When?"

"June."

She gasped, "*June?* You're telling me you haven't heard from my daughter in six months, and I'm just now hearing about this?"

"I called. I wrote. I did everything I could. I thought she just didn't want to talk to me."

"Did you come by?"

She said it like they lived down the block and he could swing past in the evening after work.

"I couldn't."

"For six months, you thought she was here ignoring you and that we were ignoring you, too, and you didn't come to see what was happening?"

"There was never a time when I had several days to drive out there and back, and I couldn't afford the plane ticket."

Every paycheck got divvied up the way it always had, even without her there. Three accounts. One for using. One for general saving. One for their future family. Without Liza's income, Nick picked up the slack, so the amount deposited didn't change, but that left him with little more than what he needed to get by. Her family wouldn't understand that. The burning embarrassment from her note crept up the back of his neck again.

"What did she say to you?"

The accusation in the question was seething. She hadn't even bothered to try to soften it. That wasn't what she was asking. What she really wanted to say was, *What did you do?*.

Nick recounted the note, told her Liza's car was missing, clothes, her toothbrush. She'd taken the bare basics of her life and walked away from his.

"That's not like her."

"I know."

"She never said anything to me about being unhappy."

"I know."

"Liza would want to talk. She would tell someone."

"Matilda. I know."

CHAPTER ELEVEN

Patient: Mary Whitman
Date: Friday, December 16, 1955
Notes:

T he patient is feeling extremely anxious about the upcoming Christmas party this weekend. This will be her first time hosting company since the accident, and she is concerned about the guests. She doesn't know what her husband has told them about her condition or how they will perceive her. She doesn't want to offend any of them by not remembering them, especially those who have been friends of the couple for many years.

The patient also expresses excitement at the prospect of spending time with more people, hoping this might be what it takes to restore her memory. Even as she says this, she seems questioning and unsure. She shares a memory she had when preparing food for the party. She does not refer to this as one of her visions or dreams but as a memory. She insists she clearly and distinctly remembers shopping for groceries during the Christmas season. After initial hope when sharing the memory, the patient becomes wary. This memory does not correspond with what her husband has shared with her *about her past, so she does not know if she should believe it. At the same time, she does not want to question everything that comes into her mind. She worries that if she does this, she will only trust what her husband has told her, and her own memories will not return.*

Very focused on memories of her family. Does not recall her parents or her siblings. Mentions her sister and seems particularly interested in remembering her since the image she had of her makes them seem very close. Hints at having had another vision of her but does not talk about it.

Mention of leaving the house makes her visibly uncomfortable.

Mary

I am awake even earlier than usual on the day of the Christmas party. Charles is still asleep when I slip out from beneath the bedspread and touch my feet to the cold floor. The shock of cold in the morning always helps to jolt my body awake, but I don't need it today. There's too much going through my mind for me to still feel tired. Smells from the party food I prepared yesterday still linger faintly behind the fresh, nose-tingling scent of cleanser that wipes each day away at the end of it. The refrigerator is bursting with gelatin molds, deviled eggs, dips, and a crystal bowl of sweet, creamy butterscotch pudding. The advertisement for Jell-O pudding that inspired it hangs from a magnet on the pink door. Before the guests arrive, I'll use vibrantly red candied cherries and gingerbread cookies broken in half to decorate the top of the bowl. Butterflies aren't particularly festive, but I couldn't resist the idea when I saw it.

The elaborate dessert I have planned for late in the evening will make up for the nod to spring. It would have been much easier if Charles had been able to find a box or two of Snowballs at the store, but he says they are the height of elegant holiday desserts, and every housewife is snapping them up as soon as they hit the freezer shelves. The ad I saw for them makes me believe it.

I'll just have to create my own. The ingredients Charles bought for me wait on the corner of the counter and in the ice box. Later today I'll scoop perfect spheres from the vanilla ice cream and put them back in the freezer to harden. Just before my guests arrive, I'll roll each in shredded coconut. A sprig of holly in creamy icing and a single candle nestled in each will add the finishing flourish.

But there will be much more on the menu before the Snowballs make their appearance. Days spent scouring magazines and exploring the recipe box on the counter crafted a list that's probably much too long. I can't bring myself to take anything away. Tonight has to be exactly right. From the tree Charles and I decorated together to the music playing in the background to every bowl and platter of food. I want my guests to be impressed from the moment they walk into the house. This is how I'll prove myself. If I can throw the perfect Christmas party, I will be a step closer to myself again.

Maybe tonight will be the night. Surrounded by friends, celebrating, and laughing. Maybe this will be what I need to bring back my memories.

While the first pot of coffee of the day brews, I go to the bathroom to get ready for the day. Just like everywhere else in the house, the window here is wavy, so anything beyond it is blurry and indistinct. There's something different about it this morning, though. Along the bottom of the pane, the glass is opaque and white. Dressed and made up, I go to the living room and look at the windows there. They all have the same white coloration along the bottom.

Snow.

I close my eyes and can feel the cold on my cheeks. The flakes touch my lips, and the clean chill fills my lungs. It's so real I want to lick my lips to gather the crystals.

But I open my eyes, and I'm staring at the thick, rippled window, the snow nothing but a stretch of white against the pane.

My husband's warm, deep voice sings from the doorway to the living room. Bing Crosby fills the room again, laced with holiday-scented excitement. I look at him, and he stops, grinning at me.

"Seems appropriate," he says. He takes a few steps toward me, and I notice the newspaper folded under his arm. "Do you think it will stick around and we'll have a white Christmas after all?"

I look back at the window.

"When was the last time I went outside?" I ask.

"Well," he says, the dreams of snow and breaths of peppermint gone from his voice, "I suppose that would be when you came home from the hospital after the accident."

I shake my head.

"That's not what I mean. The last time I was really outside. When I stood out in the yard and felt the snow. Or walked on the grass. Or listened to the cicadas."

Charles looks at me strangely.

"Walked on the grass? I can't honestly say I ever remember you doing such a thing. The outdoors aren't something you have ever enjoyed."

The heartbeat in my chest seemed to pause, then catch up in a cascade.

"What about the picnic?"

His head tilted slightly to the side.

"The picnic?"

"You told me we met at a picnic."

I watch the words click like gears through his mind until they settle into place.

"Your parents brought you. It wasn't something you wanted to be doing. I told you, Darling, they tried very hard to help you get over this resistance you have. But it seemed all their efforts only made the situation worse. We even spent most of our courtship at your parent's home. By the time we married, you didn't want to leave the house at all."

"Then how do I have friends?" I ask.

I don't mean to be arguing with him, but I can't stop the questions rushing out of me as soon as they form.

"People you knew as a child. People I introduced you to. Neighbors who come to visit."

"Neighbors?"

"Of course," he says dismissively.

"They haven't come since the accident. No one has. No neighbors. No friends. Not even my family."

I think of all the pictures he's shown me and try to find the faces somewhere else in my thoughts. Not one of them is real to me. I don't know the curves of their jaw or the sounds of their voices.

"Mary, you need to understand, what you have been through is very difficult for others. You aren't the same person you were before the accident, and it is uncomfortable for you to not remember them."

"Uncomfortable for them?" I ask incredulously. "What about for me?"

"You can't think only about yourself," he says, his voice dropping lower. "I have never gone away. I've never avoided you or turned away from you because you've forgotten our marriage. Other men would have gone to their secretaries long before now, but I've remained devoted to you because I know my wife is there somewhere. And this is what you think of me? After all I've done for you, how can you be so selfish?"

My cheeks burn and tears spring to my eyes. The taste of bile washes up on the back of my tongue, and I feel like my mouth fills with dirt. Squeezing my eyes closed stops me from toppling backward, and I nod.

"I'm sorry," I whisper. "You're right. You have been here for me. I'm sorry."

Charles's face softens, and he comes up to me, taking me by the shoulders, then gathering me close to him in a hug.

"I know you are, Darling," he whispers against my hair. "You need to trust me. I'm doing what's best for you."

I nod and pull back enough from his chest to look into his face.

"But I remember," I tell him softly. "I remember the grass and the breeze and the snow. Not from when I was a little child. More recently than that. I have these moments when I feel like I'm just about to know something, but it disappears."

71

Charles runs his hand along the side of my face and touches a kiss to the middle of my forehead.

"This is why I don't want to tell you about the projects I'm working on," he says. "It's too hard for you to differentiate between what's real and those stories."

"I don't think..."

He makes a quieting sound and shakes his head.

"That's enough, Darling. You'll talk to Dr. Baker next week, and he will help you understand. Today is for happiness and celebration. I know you have plenty to do to get ready for this evening, so get started. I have a few errands to run today, but I want to read my paper first."

He kisses me again and goes to sit in his chair. The newspaper crackles as he shakes it out and starts to read. I look at it for a long second, wondering what's strange about it. The pages are crisp. The type neatly packed along the columns. An image of children gathered around the feet of Santa sitting in an elaborate throne takes up the center of the front article. Charles leans back in his chair, scanning the inside and taking in the daily business news. It's perfect.

And that's the problem.

There's enough snow on the ground to gather in thick drifts against the window, but the newspaper is dry.

————

An hour later, Charles leaves to run his errands. Meat roasting in the oven and a pot of oranges, apples, cinnamon, and cloves sends Christmas smells throughout the house. I stand in the laundry room and pull a freshly tumbled blanket from the dryer. It feels warm in my hands, and I bring it to my face to feel the softness against my cheek.

Everything around me shifts. My senses are on the very edge, searching for something that isn't the scent of the detergent or the lingering heat of the dryer. I'm longing for something else. The smell of heat that doesn't come from metal. It's from sunshine. I close my eyes, and the fibers in my hands fill with summer daylight.

The music coming from the living room fades behind laughter. My laughter. Pure and full, from a depth within me I don't remember. But it's not just mine. Someone is laughing with me. A voice that sounds like rain. Rather than a heavy blanket meant to fold at the end of the bed, my hands feel a soft, light cotton sheet that slips through my fingers and flutters around me as I try to fold it, but strong hands pull it away and wrap it around my body. He pulls me close and presses me back against a wooden post, so the taut clothesline is overhead. Wrapped in the clean, sunbaked sheet, I eagerly accept the touch of his lips.

He doesn't taste like Charles.

The sun is too bright to see his face, but his hands touch me like they molded me, they know me so well. My body moves and shifts to fit the planes and dips of his.

Then it's gone. I want it back. I squeeze my eyes closed. I hold the breathlessness in my lungs. But there's only the blanket in my hands and The Andrews Sisters on the radio. My knees buckle, and I let them bring me down to the floor so I can rest my forehead against the cool metal of the washing machine. Heat still radiates from the dryer, warming one cheek.

Winter here. Summer there.

The faint *ding* of the timer in the kitchen forces me back to my feet. The vision left me unsteady, and it takes several steps before I can make myself walk straight.

It was more than the terrifying feeling of someone chasing me. More than seeing the precarious blonde woman across the table from me when I filled out the Christmas cards. This was different from knowing what the blades of grass felt like on the bottoms of my feet and the smell of snow when it fell through pine needles. That was a flash of something I couldn't quite put into words but could feel it deep in my bones. I knew him.

I finish the next steps of the recipes in the kitchen and gather the clean blanket to bring into my bedroom. I keep myself from looking at the door to the spare bedroom as I walk down the hallway, but that means my eyes go to Charles's study. It's closed like it always is, but something compels me to touch the doorknob. It's not the first time. When I'm alone in the house, and the crackling radio in the background or a game show droning on through the television doesn't do enough to dispel the silence, questions and curiosity creep in. I've tried the door many times when he was away at work. Not for any particular reason. I've gone into the room before. But only when he was there. It's the lock that changes things. The dynamic of a door shifts as soon as it's closed, and a lock turned into place.

Like a latched door covered with wallpaper.

The doorknob is the same smooth brass it always is, but this time when I touch it, it moves. Usually stiff from the lock that holds it in place, the knob twisting startles me. My hand falls away from it, and I take a step back. My heart drums in my chest, and my breath comes out in jagged gasps. It's like I'm waiting for something. My body is anticipating something my brain doesn't know is coming. Blood pounds in my ears then gives way to an old Christmas carol. I don't put the blanket down. Something about gripping it against my side makes me feel more confident as I step up to the door again and reach for the knob. There's a part of me that expects it to be locked now. As if I'd imagined it twisting at all. After all, I've learned not to trust myself.

But it moves. That small twist, that tiny bit of movement is enough to embolden me, and I turn the knob the rest of the way. The door swings open easily, rewarding my courage with entrance into the dim, forbidden room. Without the presence of Charles in the room, there's a different feeling. It's like he acts as a filter, ensuring I perceive exactly what he wants me to. I see what he wants me to see, and don't see what he wants to keep to himself. Now that filter is gone. The room feels like it's breathing. It's open and here and available. That's enough to almost frighten me into running out of it. But I don't.

Instead, I cross it as quickly as I can to the desk. The lamp in the corner casts a yellow glow over the dark polished wood of the surface. It's empty except for an ink blotter and silver pen perched in a holder.

Charles keeps everything put away, kept in its place. Perfect. Everything perfect. Sitting in the large chair behind the desk gives me the perspective he has of the world. I look out over the room through his eyes and see into the corners and onto the shelves. The shadows are a different depth from here.

My hands move to either side and find brass handles hanging from the fronts of drawers built into the sides of the desk. I pull them open and peer inside. The first holds an assortment of pens, paper clips, and books of matches lined carefully on the felt bottom. The other has a stack of envelopes and a book of stamps, nestled alongside a piece of wax and a seal press. I've never seen those before. I don't know why my husband would have them, but they're not what I'm looking for. I close both drawers and reach for the next two. One won't move under my hand. The other slides open to reveal several folders.

"L.B. Project," I murmur, reading the label on the folder tab.

The folder spread open on the desk; I flip through the papers inside. The pages are formatted strangely, the words scattered across them at irregular intervals and given emphasis only in some places. It takes reading through them a few times for me to realize these are the pages of a script. This is Charles's most recent project, the one he wouldn't tell me about because it was too frightening for me.

I absorb it as quickly as I can. The letters on the tab mean nothing to me. L.B. None of the characters have those initials. None of the locations share any significance with the letters. The first few pages of the story feel strange and disconnected, but that feeling fuels me on.

"Violet," I whisper, feeling the name on my lips. It doesn't feel familiar. "Benjamin."

I read the names again and again, trying to make them mean something. But they don't.

It dares me to keep going, to untangle it and find out what each single word means. I want to lose myself in it, but I can't. I've already lost track of time. Charles didn't tell me what errands he was running, so I don't know how long he's going to be gone. I can't be in here when he gets home.

The hint of horror is just beginning on the pages when I force myself to close the folder and put it back in the drawer. The locked drawer beside it torments me. I want to know what's inside, but I can't hope for him to accidentally leave it unlocked as well. Making sure there are no signs of me in the room, I carefully close the door and slip into the bedroom as fast as I can. My hand is smoothing the final wrinkle on the blanket folded across the foot of the bed when I hear the front door open.

CHAPTER TWELVE

MARY

I'm lost in a swirl of light and sound. Nothing is distinct. Nothing feels like it's really here. In the corner of the living room, the Christmas tree seems to stretch and swell, then condense down until it's nothing but a bundle of light ready to explode. The fireplace dances and sways, shedding its heat and glow through a room that doesn't need either. No one is standing near it. There are too many people crowded in the space. Too many bodies filling the air with too much heat and too much energy. I wait for the flames to jump out onto the carpet. I wait to see the fire race across the room and the windows to explode.

Charles's arm tightens around my waist before I realize my legs are swaying beneath me, catching me just before I almost fall.

"Darling? Are you alright?"

The woman we're talking to – Alice? – knits her eyebrows and drums her fingers on the side of the glass she's holding. I look from her to Charles and nod.

"Just a little warm," I tell him. "I'll just step into the kitchen for a moment."

"Do you want me to go with you?" he asks.

I shake my head, not trusting my mouth. Disentangling myself from him, I weave through the unfamiliar faces and loud conversations to the kitchen. There are guests here, too, but fewer of them. A few smile at me, and I do my best to return them. My face feels numb and stinging at the same time. Impossible weight crushes in the center of my chest at the same moment it feels like hands have grasped either side of my ribcage and are yanking it apart, splaying me open. Sweat runs down my spine and makes the nylon of my pantyhose tingle and prick against my skin.

"Mary? Are you alright?"

I don't know the voice. It was introduced to me earlier tonight. It said a name I should know. It encouraged me, nudged me, tried to force me to make a connection that wasn't there. Patricia. She lives down the street with her husband, Larry. We barbecue with them in the summer. The men grill in the backyard while she and I make lemonade and ice cupcakes with fresh strawberry buttercream.

Her voice doesn't sound like summer. I don't taste lemonade when I look at her, and there's no smell of charcoal and smoke when her husband leans close to mutter something to my husband, then laughs.

"Yes," I say with a shaky smile. "I just need a drink."

Spiced wine goes down like velvet. I down another and watch my reflection jiggle in a lime gelatin mold studded with cherries and pineapple.

"The house looks wonderful," another voice offers, like the words will give me the strength to carry on.

The reflection beside me is Deborah. She won a blue ribbon at the county fair with the strawberry pie recipe I gave her. She'd changed it only a little, braiding around the edge of the crust and sprinkling it with coarse sugar. Everyone loved it.

My tongue itches when I think of strawberries.

"Thank you." It's an obligation, not a response. I set down my glass and smile at the women coming closer to me. "I'm going to powder my nose."

The bathroom door closing behind me blocks some of the sound. I drop down to sit on the edge of the bathtub and wait for the heat I brought in with me to dissipate so I can breathe. When I feel like I can stand again, my hands press against the edge of the sink so I can look into the mirror. This is what the dozens of Polaroids Charles has taken tonight will look like. Hair hanging in stiff curls, the front swept up and rolled to the sides. Eyes wide, mascara thick on my top lashes, and black liner winged to the sides. My lips as vibrant as the cherries perched on the butterscotch pudding.

Everything screams for me to wash it off. I want to peel away the mask and see what's beneath. Maybe I'll recognize her.

I can't stay in here for the rest of the night. I want to. I want to strip out of this dress and sink into the bathtub until all the guests disappear. When they walk out with their cocktail glow and Christmas cheer and take with them their stories and memories, I'll come out. But that won't work. I have to face them. They're in my home, looking at the decorations I created, eating the menu I cooked. Judging the life crafted for me. Being a part of it is my only option.

I'm about to reach for the doorknob when footsteps just outside the door stop me. At least two people are walking down the hallway, murmuring to each other.

"What do you think is down here?" one asks.

"Bedroom?" the other says.

A third set of footsteps joins them.

"Victor, Edna. Are you enjoying the party?"

There's no hospitality in Charles's voice. It's cold and even, controlled to a sharp edge. I press close to the door, holding my breath so they can't hear it just inches away. If they look, they'll see my feet in the light beneath the door, but the tension in the confrontation is palpable. They aren't thinking about the door beside them right now.

"We were just... admiring your lovely home," the woman I assume is Edna says.

I met Edna in very brief passing when she walked in the door and looked around the house like it was the first time she had ever seen it, even though she was supposed to be one of our closest friends. Now that's confirmed.

"The party is in the living room," Charles says. "You wouldn't want the others to feel like they're missing out on something, would you?"

Victor makes a few mumbling sounds that might be words, but I can't tell over the suddenly uproarious laughter from the other side of the house. When it fades, I don't hear them on the other side of the door anymore. But when I open it, the three are still standing there. Charles is glowering at a couple with wide eyes and clothes that fit just slightly wrong. My feet stop so suddenly I nearly topple over, and my heart rises in my throat, but as soon as he notices me, Charles smiles.

"Hello, Darling. I was just showing Victor and Edna the future nursery."

My head buzzes, trying to come up with what I should say or do. It goes to the closet. The door covered in wallpaper. I force myself to smile and step up to his side, curling against it.

"It will be beautiful," I say.

They don't realize I know they're lying. They react like they were telling the truth.

"It will be so exciting for you to finally have a little one of your own," Edna says. "You will be a wonderful mother."

Charles guides me to turn around and head back toward the living room.

"Of course she will. They will be so fortunate to have her," Charles says. "But for now, it's just us adults, so who is up for a drink? Darling, are you ready to serve dessert?"

"I'll get it out of the freezer," I say.

He kisses my cheek as my eyes drift over to the window and the snow that hasn't changed.

———

Patient: Mary Whitman
Date: Monday, December 19, 1955
Notes:

But there was no hiding that they thought she was going to end up with someone different. They came from two different worlds, and Liza had passed up a type of future he couldn't have imagined so they could be together. If she had decided three years of that type of marriage is enough, and she was ready for a different path, it wouldn't have taken any explanation. She wouldn't have had to beg their forgiveness or for any favors. They would have simply settled her back into her bedroom and quietly helped her find her way.

Even with them gone, she could have gone back home. She had a key to their house, and all the little bits of cash she and Nick had hidden throughout the home would have been enough for her to buy a plane ticket. They would have come home to her going about her life and never would have had to call Nick to find out what was happening. She would have told them everything. They would have just stayed silent.

So now, he was going through the house with a different purpose. Everything had to be documented. Everything had to be examined. Everything had to be considered. It wasn't just the clothes that were missing, but the ones that were left behind. It wasn't the tiny bottle of perfume that was still sitting on the dresser; it was the bookmark she had put into the pages of every single book she'd read since the day he met her. He noticed that the first day she was gone. It was still between the pages of the thick book she'd been trying to trudge her way through because it came highly recommended. She hated that book. She had stopped on the first page and read it out loud to Nick six times before either one of them could figure out what was happening.

But she loved the bookmark. There's no reason that shouldn't have gone with her.

He had searched every hiding place she'd come up with throughout the house and found all the cash gone. Liza was exceptional at hiding money. It became like a game to her. Every time she got paid, she'd shave off a little bit and tuck it into the little unexpected pigeonholes throughout the house so it could be used when they really needed it. He went through every one and knew every bit of her careful savings was gone. But it was what he hadn't checked that bothered him now.

Rushing to the front of the house, he grabbed the handfuls of mail from the front table. Glittery envelopes and slick invitations scattered across the floor. He didn't care about any of those. It was the official envelopes he needed. Finally, he found what he was looking for. He ripped it open so fast the paper sliced through his thumb and blood spread across the white paper as he pulled the statement out and opened it up. Liza hadn't brought her credit card.

It wasn't the type of card most people use. She didn't keep it in her purse or grab it on the way out of the house every time she ran errands. It didn't hold documentation of every second of her life like other people. Instead, it was her safety net, her fail-safe. She had grown up with a father who taught her to never rely on credit. He built his wealth off the back of the wealth his father built. It was cash, assets. Never loans. Never credit. Never anything that wasn't his yet. That's how Liza had always seen it, but in some of the earliest days of their marriage, she suddenly changed her mind. A credit card appeared, and she used it once to buy groceries. She paid the bill and then tucked the card away under the false bottom of her jewelry box. The next month, she did the same. That was her ritual. Every month, she used the card once and paid it off. She was building an emergency plan for them.

If Liza knew she was walking away from their life and preparing to build her own, that would have gone with her. But it didn't. The statement showed only the groceries she bought days before she left. Nick brought the statement with him into the bedroom and dismantled her jewelry box. The card almost dropped to the floor, along with the piece of velvet that lined the hidden bottom. But it was there. The card he never touched, never used. The card he almost forgot even existed. It was there. Which meant she had nothing more than the cash she had squirreled away.

Trying to ignore the sickening aftermath of his rage still spread across the living room, Nick grabbed his coat and ran through the front door. It was only a few days before Christmas. It was the busiest time of the year to travel. But he had to hope. He had to hope that there was someone who remembered Liza. Someone who could tell him where she went or if she was with someone. Six months is a long time for someone to remember just another passenger, but that wasn't Liza. Liza was someone you didn't forget.

CHAPTER FOURTEEN

CHARLES

Charles stomped his feet against the ground, trying to warm his legs up. He brought his hands to his mouth and breathed on them. Hot air filtered down through his gloves, but it did little to thaw the chill of his skin. The temperature had dropped dramatically in the last few days, and the air felt heavy and wet, anticipating snow. He adjusted the collar of his coat close at the back of his neck and scrunched his face down, so more of his wool scarf covered it. Soon it was only his eyes that peered out over the gravel parking area. It seemed much of it had become overgrown. In the spring and summer months, grass and weeds came up through the sparsely scattered rocks, nature trying to reclaim it.

It wouldn't be that way for much longer. He would make sure it got the care it deserved. Today was the day he had been waiting so eagerly for, for so long, and now that it was finally here, every second that passed by felt long and arduous. His skin felt like electricity was dancing along it, too aware, too sensitive. Every moment that passed by, the appointed time brought him a little closer to the edge. This wasn't the way today was supposed to be. It was supposed to be perfect. Everything perfect. All the time and energy he had put into making sure this was going to happen should have made it so.

Just like Mary. So much had gone into her. So much time and effort. So much sacrifice. He had learned from his mistakes before. There were too many times when he had gone into things too enthusiastically and lost his way. It was hard when that happened. He hated to watch something he had given so much of himself to spiral out of control and have to end.

But he had Mary. She had seen his mistakes. She had seen what you learn from them. And she had seen just how far he was willing to go to make amends when something went wrong. Not that she remembered. But there was so much he didn't want her to remember. It was too much for her. Those were dark times, and she didn't deserve to have to live through them again and again just because they existed in the recesses of her mind.

She didn't know he was there that day. While she took care of their home, she thought he was running last-minute errands for Christmas. The office was closed, and he wouldn't have to go back to work for a few weeks, but this couldn't wait. In a way, he was doing some last-minute Christmas shopping. She would love it one day. Dr. Baker would help him ensure that.

He looked at his watch again. Ten minutes late. Charles had been standing there for fifteen. He could get back in his car and turn on the heater, but he didn't. When he made the appointment with Mr. McKinley, he said he would be waiting for him at noon. Proper business didn't start with a man climbing out of his car. He should be standing ready when it was time to meet and greet him with a handshake. And that's what he would do.

Finally, he heard the cracking and crunching of tires on the narrow, twisting road that led to the parking area. Mr. McKinley parked several spots away from Charles's car. It would be hard for anyone who wasn't as familiar with this space as he was to recognize that. The small stone markers that used to line one side and to help guide cars and keep them organized had long since disappeared. The fractured pieces of one were scattered in a nearby patch of grass, the only reminder of what used to be calm and control.

But Charles could still see it in his mind. He knew what it was like to see this space full, and that meant he knew that the narrow space where the elderly man who walked up to him now had pulled his worn, dust-covered white car was where he always parked. Anytime he came to the sprawling stretch of land he once loved so dearly, that was where he started his visit. It didn't matter if anyone else was there, that's where he parked. If he knew he would be coming at a time when the lot was likely to be full, someone came ahead and blocked off the area for him.

If he hadn't been late, Charles might have found the moment touching. This was probably the last time he would ever bring that car up that long road and park in that narrow spot on the crumbling gravel. A thick manila envelope clutched in one hand, told Charles Mr. McKinley hadn't changed his mind. There had been some questions a few weeks back when the old man started feeling nostalgic and hesitating to finalize the deal. But then Charles reminded him of why he had decided to sell in the first place. Then the events that made him sure he no longer wanted the massive property in his name. A few pictures and newspaper clippings took away the nostalgia and reaffirmed his commitment.

"Mr. McKinley," Charles said, extending his hand courteously.

The older man accepted it with his own. Even in the biting cold of the December afternoon, he wasn't wearing gloves. Perhaps after the years, he had spent working on this land and trying to make out of it everything he had envisioned and dreamed, his skin was immune. He no longer needed to protect it.

"It's good to see you. I'm sorry I'm a few minutes late. Christmas shopping seems to have gotten the best of some people, and the roads are almost at a standstill. Are you all ready for the holiday? Excited to see family?"

"It will just be my wife and me this year," Charles told him.

Mr. McKinley's expression dropped.

"Oh, yes. That's right. I'm so sorry."

Charles smiled and shook his head politely.

"No harm. I prefer to think of her the way she used to be as well.

One day she will be. But she is home alone right now, and I would like to get back to her."

The older man nodded enthusiastically.

"Absolutely. I completely understand. I have all the paperwork right here. Do you want to walk around and look at it? I don't think you've had the opportunity to do a full tour since it was released back into my control."

"Was there much damage?" Charles asked.

"Not much. The second fire did get to a few of the buildings on the farthest outreaches, and the investigation wasn't exactly kind to the sections of the woods and the area around the lake. But it isn't extensive, and I'm sure it can be easily repaired."

"I might like to see the lake. That's such an important feature for future development, and it's important for me to understand the full scope of any further work that will need to be done."

"Of course. All the barriers have been removed so we can just walk down there."

They made their way through overgrown grass and along neglected walkways. It had only been since the summer that Charles had been here, but it looked like it had been lying dormant for years. It was amazing how quickly a place could change when it had gone through the trials and traumas of these acres. When they got to the lake, the temperature dropped even further. Mist rolled off the surface of the black water and swirled around the weathered, gray dock jutting out into the expanse. Along the pebbled sandbar to one side, bits of yellow tape were still visible among long frozen-over footprints. Leaves and scraps of trash littered the top of the water, and a green glass beer bottle bobbed a few feet from the end of the dock.

"Have people been coming here?" Charles asked.

"A few teenagers got in here one night. An initiation of some sort. The police scared them off and put out a bulletin that anyone else seen on this property wouldn't be given a second chance. That seems to have kept them at bay."

Looking at the condition of his surroundings dampened some of Charles's spirit, but he reminded himself it was all easily fixed. He was just glad he had gotten his crews working in August. They had finished just in time for production to start again in January. This land would be revitalized, and he would bring back to the original glory he remembered. He would cherished it not only for what it was but for the fame he would soon enjoy because of it.

"I'm satisfied," he said.

Mr. McKinley grinned.

"Wonderful. Then all we have to do is sign these papers, and it's done."

They walked back up to the parking lot, and Charles opened the envelope. He read through the papers to make sure the terms had been drawn up to his liking. He signed his name and handed the pen over to Mr. McKinley, who added his own with a flourish.

"My bank will ensure the money is transferred to you by the end of the day," Charles assured him.

"You know how much this place means to me. I've owned it longer than you've been alive. Everything that's happened has been so hard on me, and it was breaking my heart to think it would be the end. I can't tell you how happy it makes me to know you will carry on the legacy. I know it's in good hands."

"It is," Charles promised. "I have dreamed of owning it for a long time. It will be well-cared-for, and I won't allow the history to be tarnished."

His eyes glittering and a sense of relief visibly lifting a weight from his shoulders, the older man shook his hand again.

"Congratulations, Alex. You are now the owner of Camp Pine Trails."

CHAPTER FIFTEEN

MARY

The first thing I did when Charles left this morning was to check his study to see if the door was unlocked. I knew the chances of him making a mistake like that twice in any length of time was unlikely, much less twice in a span of only a few days. But I still had to check. I haven't been able to stop thinking about the script pages I found in his desk. I want to know the rest of the story. There's something about it that seems familiar, like I've read about it before.

Dr. Baker is coming back today to talk to me again. It's become a routine having him in the living room, listening to me answer his questions and talk about what I'm going through. It seems like he's asking me the same things over and over. Even if I have no trouble answering him the first time he asks, he'll ask again. I feel like he's trying to guide me to something, kind of like the answer I gave him was wrong, and he wants me to keep thinking until I find the right one.

I suppose it's what he's supposed to be doing. The entire reason he's here is because of how worried about me Charles is. He never told me with as much certainty as I felt it, but I know he was as hopeful about the Christmas party as I was. It was his idea to host it this year, even after the accident. We could have canceled it. I doubt anyone would be surprised if we'd told them I wasn't up for entertaining. That possibility never crossed Charles's mind. At least, he never told me it did.

Come early November, he started talking about the party. He talked about it in much the same way as he went about most things in our daily life. He always had the assumption I would know what he was talking about. Like he could just act like it wasn't happening to me, and eventually it would go away. Not that he was dismissive. My husband has been supportive and compassionate, and it was as if he thought if he believed in me enough, my brain would simply start going along with it. It would forget all that it had forgotten and remember all there was to remember.

But it didn't work out that way. Those faces at the party the other night mean nothing to me. No, not nothing. Not really. There was a moment partway through the night when I looked over and saw a man leaned against the bookshelf, staring at me. Something in his eyes struck me, and I found it hard to turn away from him. It was like I needed to look at him, needed to see something I couldn't identify. There was nothing particularly compelling about him. His thick hair was a touch too long, and the clothes didn't quite fit into the rest of the party. There was an air about him that wasn't like the other guests. He almost seemed disdainful, like he didn't want to be there.

It wasn't just that. There was something else. Something new that wouldn't let me turn away, but also wouldn't let me say anything. We stared at each other for what felt like hours but was probably only seconds, before Charles led me away to introduce me to another group of neighbors. He called it 'reminding.'

I'm still thinking about that man. I wish I could figure out what it was about him that latched onto me so much. I can't think of his name. There are no flashes of thought that come with the look in his eyes.

The snow on the windows is gone. It must have melted overnight. I step up close to the one in the living room. It's on the front wall of the house and looks out over the street. Of course, I can't see the street itself or anything else around the house. There's only a blur, colored like the bottom of a glass with a darker streak somewhere in the middle. Pressing my face close to the glass, I try to focus beyond the waves in the window to see more detail of the outside world. It doesn't do much good. Everything remains undefined and hazy, blended into one another like an impressionist painting.

The longer I stand here, the more I'm aware of what I'm watching. Or, more accurately, what I'm not watching. There's no movement. No matter how long I stand staring through the thick, warped glass of the window, nothing changes. If a car drove down the street or a child skipped along the sidewalk, it would be a shift in the colors and shapes that could give me a loose impression of my home's place in the world. Everything remains absolutely still.

Without giving myself a chance to think, I walk out of the living room and through the entryway of the house to the front door. My fingers easily turn the little gold lock in the knob. I've unlocked this door every day, so I could get the milk from where it was delivered right at my doorstep, or gather the mail when Charles wasn't there. But it feels different opening the door without the intention of just stepping right back inside. The farthest I can remember walking along the short hallway between the two doors is halfway. There a table perfectly aligned with the gold-colored design on the rich wine and navy Oriental rug on the floor that holds the mail when there is more than an envelope or two.

I walk up to the table and run my fingers along the beaded edge of the wood. The mail hasn't come yet, so the table is empty. My eyes snap to the door at the end of the hallway. The door attached to the house is the original one. Charles had the hallway and another door added, using the privilege of inheriting his parents' millions, and the money he'd earned himself with his production company, to manipulate and adapt the house into a sanctuary for me. That door was meant to protect me, to keep me from the outside and the outside from me. The milkman stepped through it each week to leave milk, juice, and butter in its little metal crate by the second door. When he didn't use the slot to slip envelopes inside, the mailman came as far as the table in the middle to leave packages and stacks of correspondence.

So why did Dr. Baker need a key?

Each step toward the door feels like I'm walking through quicksand. The floor pulls at my feet, and everything Charles has told me since I woke up after the accident drags me back toward the house. What if he's right? The visions and dreams I've had don't make sense. If they are really memories, they should mean something to me. I should understand them or at least recognize what they could mean. But I don't. The intense image of the sun-dried sheet warming my skin as the man kissed me and the woman laughing at the table across from me seemed so real. It was like I could have touched them. Yet, I didn't know either of them.

Maybe I wasn't really remembering anything. Maybe it was just as Charles said, nothing more than my memory loss and anxiety tangling up with what he's told me about his work. Rather than really remembering my life, I'm bringing up fragments and chips of what he's described to me through our years together. Soaked in depression and tinged with fear, they create the nightmares and confusing images that have been plaguing me.

It's almost enough to let the feeling tug me back through the other door and into the living room. There are a few more presents to wrap, and I've been working on piecing a quilt I found in a basket in the bedroom closet a few months ago. That will keep me busy until it's time to make supper. Charles and I can sit on the couch together and watch *I Love Lucy* and go to bed. Maybe I'll know him this time.

My foot moves back, but I stop myself. The fast, irregular beating of my heart feels like fear and anticipation, hope and desperation, all at once. I need to see what's beyond the door. If all those people at the party live scattered through the houses along the street, and there are children to have family picnics and play at a lake I've never seen, they are out there. I had them in my home, at least the adults. They stood close to me and talked like we'd had dozens of conversations before. They exist just beyond this door. Their lives carry on without ever wondering what catastrophe will befall them as soon as they are beyond the protective recesses of their houses. Or even if they merely look through the window.

I want to know what they see.

The doorknob turns, and I ease the door toward me. My position means the door will continue to conceal me, gradually pushing me backward until I'm standing with my back against the wall and the door over me. It gives me a few more seconds of being contained. But I don't want them. Now that the door is open and I can feel air that hasn't been recycled over and over come through, I know I need to walk through it.

I do.

My first step out onto the small covered porch is surreal. I don't know what I was expecting. Something dramatic. Something that made me know I'd done something significant. Instead, the change is barely noticeable. The temperature is cooler out here, but not as much as I'd expect. I already knew the snow had melted and was no longer clinging to the window, but there was no sign of it. No slush along the side of the road. No little crystals still forming piles at the base of the bushes along the side of the house. There is no sign that there had ever been snow.

In fact, everything is pristine. It's beautiful. Almost too much so. The little white house across the street is the same as the one to each side except for blue shutters in the place of red or black. Smooth lawns look like the blades of grass had been measured with a ruler before being snipped by hand to ensure total accuracy.

But it's not the loveliness of the neighborhood that catches my attention and holds it, sending a creeping shiver along my arms and down the back of my neck. Around me, everything is silent. There isn't a whisper of wind or a single bird. Even in the middle of winter, there should be something. A cardinal or an owl, something alive in the same space as me. But I hear nothing. In the window of the house across from me, I see the outline of a Christmas tree. It's not lit, but the tinsel glints through the clear glass. Something about it sends a chill along my spine.

There has to be more than this. This is just a strange moment, an inconvenient lull. Looking out over the neighborhood from under the metal canopy of the porch is like looking into the snow globe. I'm only getting a tiny fraction, a sliver of the reality. Maybe I know more than I think I do, and that's what's bothering me. Somewhere in the back of my mind, I know it should look like something else, I just can't quite place it.

I wonder what will happen if I walk down the street. Maybe my feet will automatically take me to one of the neighbors' homes. Or maybe someone is looking out their front window right now just like I was and when they see me, they'll come out to talk to me. If it goes well, I'll do more tomorrow. I've come this far. This could be the beginning of my new life.

My hand wraps around the metal beam supporting the tiny roof over the porch. I realize I don't know what it looks like. I can only assume it's similar to the blue and white stripes of the one across the street. They make me think of blueberries with whipped cream. Or the red and white ones that look like a candy cane to the other side. The sweet-colored stripes match the shutters on each of the houses. I wonder what color my shutters are.

I start to lower myself down the first step. The moment my foot touches the concrete below, a scream cuts through the air. It reverberates around me, shattering the stillness until I can almost feel it in piercing shards against my cheeks. My hand clutches the beam so hard I feel it pressing into my palm, and I stumble back. The scream continues behind me as my leg catches the rough, uneven edge of the concrete, and I land hard on the porch. It sounds unchained and terrified, wrenching from a deep, dark place as it swells and surrounds the house. It sounds like me.

Pain moves up and down my leg like creatures with sharp claws running along my skin. I scramble for the door, pushing it open and shoving myself through a gap small enough to scrape my arm and bite into my hip. Slamming the door closed, I press my back against the wall, pressing my hands over my ears and clenching my teeth together to stop the chattering.

The world falls silent around me. I lower my hands cautiously and wait for the scream to come back, but it doesn't. Pulling myself up onto wobbling feet, I use the table to support myself for my first few steps back toward the main door to the house. It shuts with a click deep inside it. In the kitchen, the timer rings desperately, and the smell of sugar just on the edge of burning stings my nose.

Dr. Baker is only seconds away from not having cookies during our session.

Patient: Mary Whitman
Date: Tuesday, December 20, 1955
Notes:

T*he patient is particularly fixated on the windows during this session. She constantly stares at them and seems distracted when asked questions. She admits to attempting to go outside as an experiment, hoping seeing the environment would bring back memories. It was not what she expected, and describes feeling disoriented, confused, and disconnected to the surroundings. Someone screaming frightened her enough to send her back inside. Though she openly says the scream was in her voice and happened when she was going beyond her comfort zone of being close to the house; she does not admit it was her screaming and exhibits interest in attempting to go outside again.*

When asked why she would do this alone, she says she knows her husband is expecting her recovery and wants her to be able to function normally. She wants to be able to manage this on her own and show him she can 'come back'.

She has started to ask questions during her sessions as she tries to determine the meaning behind what she is seeing and thinking. She wonders if these are real memories and impressions from some point in her life, or if the combined fragility of her mind has made it so she will never be able to really differentiate what is real from what she has seen or read.

This may indicate some personal danger unless she overcomes this need.

CHAPTER SIXTEEN

CHARLES/ALEX

"Are you alright, Darling?" Charles asked, rushing into the kitchen.

He gathered Mary into an embrace before she had the time to process his arrival. The spoon she held tumbled from her hand, the thick red sauce she'd been serving slashing across the white tile and splattering across the floor. The image made his brain burn, and her eyes locked on it brought a tingling sting along the insides of his arms and into the palms of his hands. He took her by her cheeks, tilting her face, so she looked at him.

"What is it, Charles?" she asked. "What's wrong?"

"Then, you are alright? You're not frightened?"

The pink tinge that came to her cheeks told him his words were sinking in and creating a reaction. They tunneled through her and dissolved away the calm until it turned into anxiety and questions.

"Why should I be frightened?"

He pulled her against him again. One day, she wouldn't tense like this when he held her. He'd be able to hold his wife and feel her relax into his arms. There had been moments of it already. Moments when she reached into her mind and brought up memories of love and devotion, let them color the way she touched him.

"You haven't watched the news then?"

Mary shook her head, her green eyes widening, so the light from the fixture overhead sparkled in them and reflected the tile from the floor.

"No," she told him. "I've been too busy."

Charles took her hands and held them tightly in his.

"There has been a string of robberies in the neighborhood. Three houses in the last week. Someone is coming in and stealing Christmas presents and other items. The first two times, there was no one home when they went in, but at the third house, the wife was home. She was doing laundry, and a man burst into through the back door. She had left it unlocked."

Mary gasped.

"Is she alright?"

Charles's lips went into a thin line, and his eyes burned into hers. He chose his words carefully.

"She survived." Mary's hand went up to cover her mouth, and he saw her shoulders trembling. "I don't want you to worry, Darling. I've made sure you are secure here. I've added extra locks to the doors and changed the ones that were there. We'll just have to settle for our mail and milk waiting for us on the porch if I'm not here to get it for you. I don't want anyone even coming through the front door unless I'm here."

"Charles, why did you give Dr. Baker a key?"

He looked at her through narrowed eyes.

"What do you mean?"

"The mailman and milkman are able to come in and leave their deliveries right in the hallway. The first time Dr. Baker came over, I let him in, and he told me you had given him a key. Why would he need a key?"

Charles shook his head, giving her a soft smile and rubbing her upper arms soothingly.

"You must be mistaken. He doesn't have a key. There wasn't any need for him to."

She nodded, and he kissed her on the top of the head.

"I'm so glad you didn't see the news. I was so worried the whole way home that you would see the grisly story and be terrified without me here," he said.

Her eyes lifted away from the sauce spread across the counter and floor.

"You never told me what you were doing today. Did it go well?"

"It went very well. I finalized a deal I've been wanting for a long time."

"Another project?"

"Not exactly. It's a place where I spent a lot of time when I was young. The property has come under disrepair in the last few years, and the owner wanted it off his hands but was too nostalgic to make a good deal. Recent events have changed his mind, and he finally saw the benefit of selling it to me."

"Recent events?" she asked.

Charles ran his thumb across her cheekbone and smiled.

"Nothing for you to worry about. All that matters is it's done, and I think that calls for a celebration."

Mary nodded.

"Let me clean up this sauce, and supper will be almost ready."

"And I'm going to have a drink and relax. There should be a good special on tonight. Maybe something from Walt Disney. Can you believe it's been five months since that amusement park of his opened up? It feels like everyone has been waiting for it for a lifetime."

Mary didn't respond. He could hear the soft sound of her cleaning the floor and the faucet turning on to wash the spoon she'd dropped. He wondered what was going through her mind. She had seen the advertisements for the glorious achievement by the master of entertainment himself. He had created an entire world, a true fantasy, from nothing. Only his imagination and his dedication to what he knew the world should be. But she said nothing. Charles walked back into the kitchen and found her standing in front of the stove, staring into the bubbling sauce without moving.

"Mary?"

She turned to look at him.

"Yes?"

"Disneyland," he said, drawing his lips up into a smile and hoping it rose up through his eyes like water. "Can you believe it's been five months since it opened?"

"Oh. No. It doesn't seem like it."

"We'll bring our children there one day," he told her. He ran his hand along her back, feeling the buttons of her green gingham dress that so perfectly highlighted her eyes. "It will be wonderful."

"Do you really believe that?" she asked.

He looked at her questioningly. The palms of his hands twitched.

"Of course, Darling. You will get so much better. You'll see. One day soon, you will be a mother, and all this will be behind you. It will seem like a different lifetime."

———

Nick

"I know six months is a long time, but please. Can you just try to remember? It's really important."

The woman's face perfectly fit into the round opening in the bulletproof glass of the ticket counter. She sighed heavily. It was a burdened sigh that carried too many frustrated passengers, cold forgotten dinners, and a Christmas that would probably be spent trying to sleep off getting ready for it. Nick didn't care. It didn't matter to him who he was inconveniencing or how. All that mattered was Liza. He'd lost so much time already, and the police weren't doing shit to help him. Every one of them looked down their noses and licked crumbs from their lips as they listened to him. They didn't even have the decency to stop stuffing Christmas goodies from cheerful tin boxes and muffin baskets down their throats to hear what he had to say.

This was a prime time of year for them. They got to march along parade routes scattered with crepe paper and tiny candy canes and puff out their chests while handing out presents to children. Every day bootlickers and single women, or sometimes not single women, whose panties got wet thinking about their handcuff fetishes and hero complexes swooped in with baked goods. It was just too much for them to think about to give an instant of thought to Liza.

"She left a note?" they asked.

"Yes."

"Saying she was leaving?"

"Yes."

"And she took her belongings?"

"Yes."

"And money?"

"Yes."

"So, what exactly is it that you want us to do?"

"She didn't leave on her own," Nick insisted.

Another nod and another bite of cinnamon roll. He went through the whole story three more times.

"Poor sap's wife left him, and he can't deal with it," one of them muttered to another as Nick walked out twenty minutes later.

At least the doe-eyed woman at the desk helped him fill out a missing persons report. She wouldn't look directly at him when he handed it back over. He knew what that meant. It was a cursory gesture, but the officers might get a moment to look at it over a box of Valentine's Day conversation hearts. If then.

He was going to have to look for her himself, and that's exactly what he was doing.

"When did you say she left again?" the woman asked.

Nick tried to stop himself from exploding. He'd already answered the question four times.

"June," he told her. "She's blonde. Big eyes. Here. Look at the picture again."

He held his phone up to the window to show her the image of Liza. It was his favorite picture of her, a candid shot of her curled up on the porch swing of the miniscule bed and breakfast where they'd spent their anniversary. Bare feet and a thick sweater, her head tilted back. She was laughing at something he said. Nick couldn't remember what it was. It didn't really matter. The laugh was all that he cared about. He could still hear it, still feel it washing over him.

"And you know she took a train out of here?"

Nick's fingers clenched the edge of the counter.

"No," he said through gritted teeth. "I don't know that. I don't know anything. I'm trying to figure out what happened to her."

"Six months is a long time to remember someone passing through here."

He pushed away from the counter, nearly knocking over the man standing behind him close enough to hear their conversation, not even trying to hide that it was exactly what he was doing.

"Thank you for your help."

"Merry Christmas," the woman said after him with as much enthusiasm as she might tell him the vending machine only took cash.

Nick didn't stop. His next destination was the bus station. Rows of gleaming Greyhounds waiting outside the sprawling terminal for holiday travelers to stuff themselves inside. The carpeted seats would soon feel damp with sweat, and the interior would smell like people and food and impending snow.

Liza hated the bus. She'd much rather ride the train with the swaying cars and the endless aisle she could roam along if she felt like it. But it hadn't stopped her from booking tickets on a trip that left the city in the middle of the night and took four hours longer than driving because it was cheap, and it meant they could sit in the far back under a blanket and celebrate three months of marriage away. Even if it was only one state away. Even if they stayed at a terrible hotel and ate nothing but pizza and delivery Chinese food from the bed for two days before tucking right back under that blanket and going home.

Liza wouldn't choose to come here by herself and travel alone in the too-cold air conditioning with the too-naked passengers. But someone else might choose it for her. If they wanted to get away quickly and easily, a bus was an easy way to do it. Technically, every passenger was supposed to present identification with their ticket when getting on. Nick knew enough about bored workers and lack of professional give-a-damn to know that wasn't how it always worked. He also had the anecdote of presenting a Pizza Inspector ID badge complete with a goofy picture he'd snapped on a kiddie ride at Chuck E. Cheese during his sophomore year of college to prove it. If it was busy enough and the person on duty was bad enough at their job, it wouldn't be a major challenge to push past with only a cursory wave of a card.

But her ID wasn't in the house, either. It was entirely possible this wasn't a sudden, random event, and they actually bought a ticket in her name.

He didn't know what could have happened then. Liza wasn't delicate. She wasn't the type of woman to just sit idly by if someone was trying to hurt her. She wouldn't go down without a fight. That's what scared him. What happened after the fight?

Even though he knew it would be futile, he went back by the police department before going home that night. No one at the bus or train station, or the airport, remembered seeing Liza. But they were just people. There wasn't even a way of guaranteeing they were the ones who were working the day she left. If the police requested surveillance videos from the cameras that lurked in every corner and on every wall in public areas like transportation stations, they might catch a glimpse of her. The suggestion ended up jotted on a torn piece of paper tucked in a flimsy folder with his missing persons report.

Nick went home and cleaned up. Every shard of glass brought tears down his cheeks.

CHAPTER SEVENTEEN

MARY

I dream of a castle and wake up crying. Before I know what brought on the tears, the rest of the dream disappears like wisps of smoke, and I'm left with nothing but the damp pillowcase and Charles snoring beside me. The sun isn't even up yet. A chill makes the air feel like thin sheets of ice as I move carefully out from under the blankets and get out of bed. I don't want to move too quickly and wake him up. Any minute now, the furnace will come to life and knock off some of the cold. I'll be able to breathe without my lungs aching.

Charles insists on keeping the temperature of the house close to freezing at night. He says it's good for our health. There's a newspaper article on it somewhere in one of the books in the living room. He brought it out at the beginning of the season when I tried to inch the thermostat up just a few little notches.

The robe closing around me momentarily makes me colder as it holds the frigid air against me, then it starts to warm up. I creep down the hallway and into the kitchen. There should be moonlight here. The huge window above the sink should let beams like liquid mercury flow through and sparkle on the faucet, illuminate the tiles, glow on the pink refrigerator door. But there's only inky darkness and a faint glimmer of light from a weak electric candle that is perched on the windowsill, welcoming no one. The light from the bulb blocked by the thick wood.

I plug in the strand of lights around the Christmas tree to burn away a little more of the darkness. Turning on the main light might wake up Charles. But this is enough. The little multicolored lights are plenty to see by as I pull the large photo album out from the bottom of the stack of albums beneath the coffee table. It's the one I've looked through the least. Probably because of how thick and overwhelming it is. The others are thinner, with far fewer pages. It's easier to try to soak in faces and events and places when it comes in smaller doses. This last album is monstrous. Holding it in my lap feels like holding my whole life in my hands.

That's essentially what Charles says it is. This is memories of my childhood, our courtship, even our wedding. I remember that surprising me the first time he said it. I'd imagined an entire album dedicated to the wedding and page after page of white organza and stiff tulle. Instead, it's a collection of pictures arranged over just a few pages. An A-line cotton dress. A cake served from the kitchen table. The images are all discolored and strangely taken, blurred like whoever took them was moving while trying to snap the moments.

I didn't pick up the album to look at the wedding. At least, not the backs of Charles and me as we stand in front of some large stone fireplace on a bright blue carpet saying our vows. And not us feeding each other, barely visible under the veil the photographer must have playfully draped over our heads to cocoon us both. I'm looking at the guests.

None of them are looking at the camera. The colors of the pictures are warped, altered by the film, so the punch they sip looks noxious pink, and everything white might be glowing. They're all leaned toward each other in conversation or gazing away from the camera as they eat. There is one of Charles dancing with a woman who might be his mother, but her head is on the other side of his, so the only thing I can see is the navy blue dress and dyed matching shoes. I flip through every one of the pictures, and then go back and flip through them again.

Not a single one has someone looking directly at the camera. Yet everyone is posing. The positions are unnatural. No one's back is that straight when they are leaning toward someone to speak. No one holds a canape that carefully while eating it. But I can look past that. I can tell myself they were at a wedding and very conscious of being photographed. What I can't look past is the man standing in the back of several of the pictures.

His blonde hair hangs close to his eyes. He talks to no one.

Spreading the album on the table to hold its place on that picture, I go to the sideboard where a stack of new Polaroids sits. They're the pictures Charles took the night of the Christmas party. I carry them back to the table and sit on the couch, pulling my cold legs under me. My hands shake slightly as I go through the pictures, examining each of them. They are black and white, but far clearer than the wedding pictures. Finally, I find the one that's been stuck in my mind.

The cold-eyed blonde man who stood by the bookshelf and stared at me. His eyes are just as piercing in the picture as they were when they caught hold of me from across the room. The washed-out color of the image only makes them more menacing. My stomach turns, but I force myself to look at it again. I set the picture down next to the album to compare the two images. It's not exact, but the wedding pictures are lower quality. Picking up the party picture again, I flip through the next few pages of the album and do another comparison. More pages and another. More pages and another.

He's always there. His dishwater hair. His unnerving eyes. He's there.

The wedding.

My family's Easter dinner.

Charles's father's retirement party.

Another Christmas.

Fourth of July.

He's there. The caption never mentions his name, and he's never in the front of the picture. Always in the back, filling in space, creating a reality with his presence. Gathering up the stack of pictures, I bring them back to where they were. They sit in the exact same spot they were when I picked them up, the right one on top. Charles will notice if they change.

The furnace turns on as I cross the room again and take my place back on the couch. I don't need it as much anymore. My face burns, the heat sharp and prickling as it moves along the sides of my neck. Going back to the beginning of the album, I carefully go over each page again. This time, I'm not looking for the man by the bookshelf. I don't know who he is or what about him makes my blood go cold. All I know is he was in too many pictures, at too many events for me to not have been introduced to him during the party. For someone to be at that many family functions, he should have come up to me and greeted me.

But I'm putting him aside for now. There's another face I'm looking for in the pictures. A face that should be there. Maybe it is. Maybe I just don't remember ever seeing the dynamic golden-haired woman with bright eyes and a wide-mouthed, honest laugh. The way Charles talked about her wasn't mean in any way, but it also wasn't particularly warm and loving. It's possible there is some sort of rift between the two of them, and he didn't feel like sharing many stories about her in all the times we've been through these albums together. She just didn't seem important. Maybe she's here.

But she's not. My sister. The close-knit sibling I haven't seen because of her war-wounded husband and their small children. The sister I wrote Christmas cards with and grew up alongside. She isn't in any of the pictures. My fingertips run over the captions written beneath each of the pictures.

Mary's mother and father.
Celebrating Easter with Mary's family.
Mary's brother, Avery.
Mary with her father.
But not a single mention of Vivian.

I look at the picture of my father and me again. We're in what looks like a wood-paneled recreation room, sitting on either side of a marred green card table. Each of us is leaned over the table and concentrating intently on a partially finished jigsaw puzzle in front of us. I look to be around twelve years old. I flip to another picture. Several years later, I've lost the gangly body of my preteen years and am taller, my head nearly to my father's shoulder. We're standing with our backs to the camera as we string a congratulatory banner across the front of the same large stone fireplace where my wedding pictures are set.

My father looks exactly the same. Dark hair. Dark mustache. Thick hair on his arms. In the next, he looks the same. Over the course of the years that passed during those pictures, he didn't change. Not a single gray hair. No difference in the style. Going back to the pictures of Christmas with my family, I stare at one that stands out to me. My mother and father standing on either side of a Christmas tree. Closing my eyes, I try to remember that moment. Nothing appears. I focus on just my father. With so many pictures of us, we were obviously close when I was young. There should be an imprint of him deep inside me. The smell of his aftershave or the way his mustache felt when he hugged me.

Still nothing.

I turn my focus instead to my mother and try to imagine her hugging me. She should smell like fresh baked bread and flowers. But I don't know. I can't feel her arms around me. I can't imagine standing beside her in the kitchen, learning to cook so one day I would be ready for my own husband and children.

Opening my eyes, I look at the picture of the Christmas tree again, then I stand and walk over to the mantle. The silver frame feels cool and heavy in my hand. Turning it over, I carefully move aside the little black pieces of metal that hold the cardboard piece in place. It releases the matte that holds the photo and then the photo into my hand. I bring it with me to the table and set it upside down as I carefully peel away the adhesive sheet over the album page. The picture of my parents is sticky and difficult to pop away from the yellowed paper, but I manage to wriggle it free from the cardstock corners that hold it.

My hand shakes as I flip the picture over and set it beside the one of Charles and me. I stare down at them for a few seconds before slowly turning them over again so I can see both images. The tree is identical. Not just a Christmas tree. Not even just a Christmas tree with ornaments and strung with tinsel. A tree with scrawny branches and exactly placed strands of tinsel, with ornaments on the same boughs and the same whittled wood star on top. A tree with a shadow at its base that doesn't match with where I'm standing and that I never noticed because of the matte in the silver frame.

Turning the pictures back over relieves me of looking at them, but it brings me face to face again with the numbers stamped into the backs. A sequence that indicates when the film was manufactured. It's the same. Which means the two pictures, one taken when I was just a child and one when I had just gotten married, were taken on the same batch of film.

Slowly I turn the pictures over one more time. My fingertips run over the pictures, and I feel like tiny fragments of broken glass fall into place in my mind. It's incomplete, only bits of words and fractured flashes. The images of my wedding with their highly saturated coloring must have been sent away for processing. Such a special occasion warranted the extra time it took to take the pictures and then send them to be developed. But the two Christmas pictures are different. Their shape is different. The feel of the material between my fingers is different. These were taken by an instant camera like the one Charles carried around during the Christmas party and used to produce the stack of black and white images sitting on the sideboard.

The fragments in my mind are pulling together. It's labored and wavering, unsure of itself as much as I am unsure of it. My fingertips continue to run along the image, touching each ornament, tracing the strands of tinsel. They pause over one of the faces, and a rush of vibrant, intense reality fills my mind. I can see my father smiling at me. I can feel that smile all the way into my heart and remember it from when I was just a little girl. My father is joyously sharing his collection, the one frivolity he won't give up no matter how much my mother narrows her eyes at him or gives big, meaningful sighs.

My red-headed, smooth-faced hobby photographer of a father who has just told me about his prized possession as a teenager... the first color instant camera invented in 1963.

CHAPTER EIGHTEEN

MARY

A sound in the back of the house brings my stomach up into my throat. Charles is awake and shifting around in the bedroom. Moving as fast as I can with shaking hands, I put the picture of us next to the tree back in the frame and set it on the mantle, then rush back to the couch. The picture of the people he's been calling my parents for six months is back in place, and the adhesive sheet just smoothed over it when Charles shuffles into the living room.

My husband.

Thinking the words is like droplets of acid on my tongue.

He hasn't dressed yet. I haven't checked the time, but now that I'm paying attention, I notice the room has lightened some. It's after sunrise, but still early enough for Charles to be comfortable moving around the house in his black slippers and pajamas. I'm sitting on the couch with the album in my lap, turning the pages and letting my eyes slide over each of the pictures. He doesn't know I'm barely even processing the images or that I'm carefully watching him out of the corner of my eye. My body tenses as he walks across the room to the mantle and reaches up for the silver frame. He shifts it slightly, adjusting its angle just barely, but enough to make the muscles in his face less tense when he turns to me.

"You're up early," he says.

"I'm just looking at the albums," I tell him.

My brain is churning, my stomach feeling like it's being turned inside out. But I have to stay calm. I keep the honey dripping from my voice and the innocence in my eyes. Until I understand what's happening, he can't know what I remember.

Charles sits down beside me and leans close enough to press our arms to each other. I'm thankful for the thick layers of fabric that prevent our skin from touching.

"You woke up before the sun to come look at photo albums?" he asks with a soft laugh.

The chaos in my mind unravels as a sense of calm comes over me. I have only one option. Twist him around my finger.

"I think I'm starting to remember," I tell him.

His eyes light up, and he leans a little closer.

"Really?" he asks.

I nod.

"It started at the party. Edna and Victor. As soon as I saw them, they felt so familiar to me. It was like they belonged in our house. Over the last few days, I've been thinking more about that and realized I haven't looked at these albums in several weeks, but I'm seeing faces in my mind."

"Faces?" he asks. "What do you mean?"

"Faces," I repeat, then look down at the random page in the album spread out in front of me. "These faces. I will be in the middle of doing the dishes or folding laundry and something comes into my mind of one of them. I thought maybe it was just remembering these pictures, but maybe it's more than that. Like this," I point to a woman in one of the pictures. "The caption says it's the Fourth of July and we are having a cookout. I remember this woman brought a patriotic Jell-O mold and set it down right next to the lime one I had made, and the cherry one Edna made. We laughed and laughed. It was so funny seeing all those glittering molds sitting on the table together."

against the wall, I put the other one on top to hold it back down and cover the look of the peeled tape.

When I'm satisfied it looks untouched; I move to the closet. My compulsion is to close the bedroom door, but I'm worried if I do, I won't hear if Charles comes home. I open the closet door and see the slight depression of the wallpaper, and the subtle tear from where my hand pressed the paper against the door is still there. I take one more glance over my shoulder and lean forward to touch the latch again.

I can't just tear the paper away. Even if there is nothing behind that door, Charles wouldn't be happy to see the paper ripped from the wall. He went to a tremendous trouble to cover the door seamlessly. That wasn't by accident or just an after-thought for him. This was intentional and deliberate. Feeling the edge of the door, I know ripping the paper here would be evident, too. Instead, I move to the edge of the wall. The way he hung the paper isn't like in other rooms. It's not flat against the surface and pasted down. He hung it so the center of the paper bubbles out over the door and creates the illusion of a flat wall. That means there is enough paper to carefully peel away from one side without having to tear it completely.

It feels like it takes forever as my fingertips slowly loosen the paper from the corner where the side and back wall come together and lift it away. Finally, it is too high above me to keep going. Instead of trying to reach, I kneel down on the floor and begin along the bottom edge. Finally, I have a piece hanging enough to lift it up over the door without tearing it. I don't know how much time has passed or how short my minutes are ticking down. But I can't stop. Not this time.

Lifting the paper up, I drape it over the clothing bar and use the hanger with the sequined dress to hold it in place. The door is right in front of me, fully exposed. I touch the latch. It feels more significant now that I can touch it while also looking at it. The metal feels oddly warm when I touch it. It moves easily, like it hasn't been long since the last time someone opened the door. A gust of cold air gushes from the open space as the thin square of plywood creaks open on its flimsy hinges.

Every house has a crawlspace. It's the veins of the house where air and dust, breath and voices flow from one room to the other. Every house has a crawlspace. But not one filled with suitcases, duffel bags, and purses. The sight of them makes my breath stick in my chest. I can't force it out, but I can't draw it in. It starts to ache as I reach for the closest bag. It's cold to the touch and brings the chill with it as I pull it out of the crawlspace and onto the floor of the closet with me. The zipper hesitates just slightly as I lead it over the top of the gray fabric. Inside are stacks of neatly folded clothes, and what looks like a handful of hastily added panties. A plain beige bra takes up one corner, and a pair of stilt-like high heels pushes the fabric out on the other side.

I sift through everything inside and find only more clothes.

Flipping the bag closed, I reach for another. Inside, the items are similar. Basic closing, undergarments. But they're strange and unfamiliar. Small. Darkly colored jeans, t-shirts, thin blouses in bright colors. Short skirts and scraps of lace. A suitcase contains much the same. Now I reach for one of the purses and set it in front of me on the floor. Before I open it, I reach for another and then the third. Set out in a row in front of me, their differences are obvious. A range of sizes and styles, obviously not the collection of one woman.

A gold clasp holds the first closed. Loosening the clasp, I lift the black leather and reveal the contents. A ponytail holder, a few cellophane-wrapped pieces of hard candy, loose tissues, a tube of lip balm. There's little inside to get any hint to who owns the purse or why it ended up in the crawlspace. As I close it and push it aside, I notice a tag dangling from the handle. It's monogrammed with a large 'M'.

I quickly open the second and dig through makeup, torn papers, and several loose keys. There's no wallet, no checkbook. Feeling around the liner, I find a narrow flap concealing a delicate hidden zipper. Inside is a small pouch. My fingers flip it inside out, and I find a folded piece of paper inside. The torn piece of paper has only a few words on it.

Liza,

Don't forget Wednesday afternoon. 3rd.

T he third purse is small and brown made of woven leather. It has the fewest items of the three, containing only a hair clip and a narrow silver bracelet caught on the inside of the zipper. I loosen it and flip over the curved rectangular panel held by a fragile chain.

To my daughter,
Happy Sweet Sixteen

M . *Liza. Daughter.*
M. Liza. Daughter.

It keeps repeating through my head, a constant stream that gets louder and louder until it's pounding in my ears like the blood my heart pumps out. It hammers my throat and eardrums and head and eyes so fast and hard, I feel sick. Frantic now, I drag more out of the crawlspace. A bag of shoes far too small for my feet. A pile of empty picture frames. A stack of books. My breath feels painful and short again as I pull the last items from the unfinished floor and set them on my lap. Photo albums.

Easter.

Christmas.

Birthdays.

Fourth of July.

Anniversaries.

Charles. Charles. Charles. Charles. Charles.

Different women. Different *wives.*

The same pictures.

A voice in the back of my mind tells me to stop as my hand lifts and reaches back inside the crawlspace. It sounds like a scream.

My fingertips touch the first book on the stack, hesitate for only a second, then pull it toward me. A woman on the front reclines against a large rock as she reaches for the man standing above her. She could just as easily be fearing for her life, warding him off with the delicate, pale hand lifted over her face. But the dress stretched low over her breasts, and the shirt hanging from his wrists behind his back indicate desire.

How easily the two can be confused.

The pages crackle as I open the book and glance at the feathery fine print on the back of the cover page. They feel old and worn to my touch, the spine broken and lined with a web of white breaking through the dark blue from being read dozens of times. An old, well-used book with a copyright date fifty years in my future.

The doctors said when my memory comes back, it will either be in a trickle or a wave. Instead, it falls like snow. Gentle and slow, gradually building until it's so thick I can't see anything else.

Sweat beads on the base of my skull and drips down the back of my neck. Summer heat presses in around me. The smell of dirt fills my nose and creeps along my tongue until I can't speak through the taste of mud. Pain radiates from the side of my head down one side of my neck. My eyes open. Blades of vibrant green grass cross my line of vision, but in front of me a shape looms low to the ground. Charles, his suit jacket draped across the top of the fence, digging into the ground. At his feet, a swirl of tangled blonde hair, tinged with streaks of red. All around me, the smell of roses.

CHAPTER NINETEEN

NICK

This was the last place he wanted to go. It had been a relief to walk away from the camp six months ago, and even though he knew there was always going to be a time when they would have to go back, Nick wanted to stretch those days as far as he could. Boss was never going to let it go. He was never going to admit the project was doomed from the very beginning and needed to just be allowed to fade away. It would always be a part of him that believed he could create magic out of the story of Camp Pine Trails. He wanted desperately for the curse to be real. He never told anybody that, of course. The Boss was far too buttoned-up and level-headed to admit to believing something like a supernatural force taking over that summer camp.

But Nick had seen it in his eyes. All those days they spent preparing for the filming and during the long weekend, before it all went wrong, before the loss and madness and death and fire. He'd watched as Boss got wrapped up in the story the original campers whispered around the tables in the mess hall. Talks about the girl going missing. The girl who disappeared fifteen years ago and was never seen again. Some people were afraid of the camp after that.

They thought there was something there. It only got worse when people started disappearing again and blood appeared in the woods.

Nick never believed in a curse. He never thought there was anything more than a godforsaken, crumbling old summer camp that should have been put out of its misery decades before. But even he got chills when he remembered the storm that night. The sound of Lisanne Banes's scream. Tendrils of black hair across the sand.

The police claimed it, then. Even the owner of the property wasn't allowed to step foot on it without at least two officers with him. The entire production shut down without any word of how long it would take for the land to be released again. It was so soon after Liza left, and Nick was still caught up in the midst of trying to replace Vanessa, the actress who walked away. She believed in the curse, too. He'd packed up his camera equipment, cleared out the creaking, spider-filled cabin where they'd been sleeping and left the camp happily. Maybe the police would never let Mr. McKinley have it back. Or if they did, maybe Mr. McKinley would be smart enough not to allow the production company to come back and create more trouble for him and the camp.

Nick had heard someone was in the market to buy the land and turn it into a resort. They would level the old cabins and add in luxury bungalows. A gleaming restaurant and bar would replace the mess hall, and fresh, rejuvenated versions of the activities would take the place of the aging fields for those who wanted to recapture their youth. Mr. McKinley should let that happen. He'd hung onto the camp for so long, taking over for his father and his father before him. There was no one else in the McKinley line to pass it to now. The camp had been his devotion. He'd had no children. It was time to move on.

But the hope of never having to see this place again shriveled that morning when he got a call from The Boss saying he needed to see him. The office was closed. They didn't have any hours scheduled or project meetings until January. The writing team had already finished the script rewrite and sent it to him for approval. There was no reason he should need to see him. But Boss insisted. Nick agreed before he knew where he was meeting him. Hope of eventually making something of himself and finding the success he had been pursuing for years to prove himself to Liza got him in the car and on the road.

Not going would be giving up on her. He would never do that.

The big powder blue car was already in the parking lot when Nick wound his way up the narrow, twisting pathway to the aging gravel parking area at the front of the camp. It looked even eerier now that it was totally empty. Somehow it was starker than it had been even before they started filming, and he visited with the rest of the crew. The camp looked tired, beaten down by everything that had happened to it.

The Boss was grinning when he climbed out of the car and walked toward Nick. Nick noticed an envelope gripped in his hand and wondered what this was all about. Was it possible this was what he had been waiting for? He was finally going to get the promotion and raise Nick had been angling after, and Boss had decided to make it a spectacle by bringing him out here to give him his contract?

"Good to be back, isn't it?"

Nick tensed at the words even though he didn't mean to.

"Not particularly," he answered.

There was no reason for him to lie about it. No one else on the crew except for a few of the stragglers at the bottom of the food chain, who fed off Boss's crazy, actually enjoyed being here. For them, it was some sort of artistic spiritual experience. For the rest of them, it was creepy as hell and the fodder for at least three grown men sleeping with nightlights.

A big, self-satisfied grin told Nick his sentiments weren't taken seriously.

"Oh, come on," Boss said. "You just don't remember how amazing it was. You're thinking about all that police unpleasantness."

"Several people going missing or dying seems like more than just unpleasantness," Nick muttered to himself.

"Let's take a quick walk."

"I really need to be getting home."

I really need to be searching for my wife.

"Just a quick one. There's something I want to show you I think you will be very interested in seeing."

The spark of anticipation returned, and Nick fell into step as they headed onto the walkway that led deeper into the camp. He felt a chill surround him that had nothing to do with the bitter December temperature. More of it came up off the water, and he felt his steps slow as Boss turned toward the lake, but he pushed on. They walked out onto the dock, and Nick had to grab hold of the support to hold himself steady. He never wanted to see this lake again. Not after that horrible morning and the corpse that rode in with the water.

"What are we doing here?" Nick asked.

He'd been focused on the wooden slats at his feet, but now he looked up at the end of the dock and the man looking out over the water. An image flashed in front of his eyes of the same man sitting on a folding chair in that same spot, looking at sunlight on the water and waiting for a woman to climb into the canoe bobbing at the end of the dock.

"I told you, there's something very exciting I want to show you. Come out here and look at the lake."

Nick released the wooden beam and took the few strides down the dock. The image came again. Grinning as he showed a picture of Liza in her Halloween costume to one of the other crew members. Flipping it to the next picture, one of her smiling at him from across the table at breakfast on her last birthday. Placing the phone into the curious hand reaching around the chair toward him.

"What are we looking at?" he asked through the twisting feeling forming low in his stomach.

"My lake."

The same grey eyes that winked at Nick now had stared at his phone then. Six months ago, as they sat on this dock and waited for Lisanne Banes to shoot her scene rowing across the lake in the canoe. They stared at Liza like they'd never seen her, like she was suddenly something new to him.

"What?"

It was a contract in the folder, but not for Nick. Not for the promotion onto the main team he'd been waiting for and grinding himself into the ground to earn for years. It was to purchase the camp.

"It's mine. I bought Camp Pine Trails."

"You bought it?" Nick asked incredulously. "I thought someone had been putting in interest about it because they were going to turn it into a resort."

Another wink and Nick's fist ached to wipe the grin off his face.

"All mine. It will need some work, of course. But it will live on forever. A legend."

Nick looked down at the contract in his hands, at the signature looped dramatically on the line above Mr. McKinley's name. Disgust writhed through him. No longer The Boss. No longer a joke.

Charles Alexander Whitman.

Alex.

The man obsessed with Nick's wife.

———

Alex/Charles

The look on Nick's face had been strange when Alex showed him the freshly signed contract. Alex had expected him to be surprised but in a good way. Not stone-eyed and shocked.

He should have expected it. Of all the people on the team who had been involved in the Bethany Project, Nick had been the most enthusiastic. He had eagerly worked with the actors and even built up a rapport with Lisanne Banes, Bethany's best friend. Possibly too much of a rapport for a married man and a married woman. The corners of Alex's mouth turned down at the thought, but he pushed it away. Nick was just envious. He wouldn't admit it, but he admired the camp as much as Alex did and would have longed to have something like it for himself.

After all, he was going through an incredibly difficult time. His wife had walked out of their home and their marriage, and Christmas was only a few days away. He could commiserate with him. It wasn't the same with Mary. She was still there. He could still hug her and hold her and tell her stories about their life so she would internalize them and make them her own. But he did know what it was to lose a wife. It could be a challenging adjustment, no matter what the circumstances.

Nick would come around. He'd come to understand that marriages don't work out sometimes, and it's usually for the best for both the husband and the wife to just let go and move on. There are others on the horizon, and life can continue. He'll eventually see that Alex owning the camp will be a good thing for everyone. Soon the film would be in production again, and the new script would make a masterpiece. The camp would be flocked with people wanting to see and experience it, and anyone attached to it would reap benefits.

That's why Alex wanted to share it with Nick first. The man could use a boost after the year he'd had and the rough few weeks ahead. He needed something to look forward to and a bit of hope to carry him through.

But it was the look on his face that stopped Alex. Nick had been cold, his expression unreadable as he stared Alex down, then grumbled he had somewhere he needed to be and left. Alex was still sitting in his car in the gravel parking area of the camp. He'd been working on finding his own spot like Mr. McKinley had. He didn't want to just take over that spot as his own. That was for the owner of that era of the Camp Pine Trails. Alex needed a place of his own for this new era.

His favorite Christmas song came on the radio when he cranked the ignition, and he paused. Not wanting to miss any of it in the crunching of the gravel under the car tires, he sat back and let the music fall over him. After a few seconds, he reached into the passenger seat and picked up his briefcase. Popping it open, he took out another folder and slipped the papers into his hand. His eyes rolled over the words typed neatly onto the page.

"Patient, Mary Whitman," he murmured. "Date, Monday, December 19, 1955..."

CHAPTER TWENTY

MARY

I wait for Charles just inside the door. I haven't been greeting him this way when he gets home in the last few days, and I can tell he misses it. The dull thud of the first door closing confirms he's home. My palms sweat. Footsteps come toward the second door. My heart pounds in my chest, and my breath feels labored, but I force it to slow. I hear the key in the locks, disengaging them.

One.

Two.

Three.

As the door glides open, I lift my arms. He comes into the house, and I step forward, closing the space between us, wrapping my arms around his neck.

"Hello, Dear. Welcome home."

Charles doesn't hesitate to wrap his arms around my waist and accept the embrace. It's what he's been waiting for since I woke up. Probably long before then.

"Hello, Darling," he smiles. "You seem to be feeling much better."

"Yes," I say with a nod, interweaving my fingers in front of me and swaying just enough back and forth to make the thick petticoats and crinoline under my skirt swish. "Supper will be ready in just a few minutes. I wanted to make something extra special for you tonight. Why don't you go wait in the living room, and I will make you a drink?"

He shrugs out of his coat, and I take it along with his hat to hang on the coatrack.

"That sounds wonderful. I'll just bring my briefcase to my study first."

He leans in for a kiss, and I tip my face up toward him. The sound of his voice is like bourbon. The touch of his lips is like the aftermath. My smile is rehearsed, but it's enough to fool him. He walks down the hall to the locked door of his study humming a Christmas song. He doesn't realize it's one he shouldn't know, one that wouldn't play on the antique radio in the living room for another three years.

He's slipping.

The key to the study emerges from its cozy spot in his inside pocket, and he makes quick work of releasing the lock and returning the key to its place. I go to the living room and have his drink ready for him when he comes in, dropping into his chair with a heavy sigh.

"Did Santa Claus keep you very busy this afternoon?" I ask playfully.

He chuckles through his first sip. The olive bobs around at the bottom of the glass. It doesn't want to get near his mouth, either.

"No. His tasks for me were very quick. What took the most time was going out to that new property I purchased."

"Is there something wrong with it?"

"Oh, no. Nothing wrong. Don't you worry your little head. I just wanted to share the good news with an employee."

"Speaking of your employees, there's something I'd like to do for them."

Charles looks surprised, his eyebrows rising in a questioning expression.

"Oh?"

"Well, it is nearly Christmas, and so many of them weren't able to attend our party. I want them to know how much we appreciate them and that they are valued, particularly at this special season."

His eyes soften, and he nods.

"You are absolutely right. You see, that's why I need you, my darling wife. I think so much about business and working I forget to see the value of all the people who help me. This is the perfect time of year to make sure they know they are remembered. What did you have in mind?"

I perch on the arm of his chair and absently run my fingers through his hair.

"I know you've been doing so much and deserve some time to just relax, but to do the plan I have, I'd really need your help."

He looks into my eyes, and I lower my eyelashes, touching my bottom lip just slightly with the tip of my tongue. Not enough to be truly suggestive, but enough to give him a hint that keeps his attention locked on me and not my fingertips trailing down along the side of his neck.

"What do you need?"

His eyes watch my tongue, and his hand runs up and down his thigh.

"Will you go to the store for me? There are just a few ingredients I don't have. I mean," I look down again, letting my fingers move a little further and making sure I'm aligned just right so he can glance down the neckline of my dress. "I could try to do it myself. Dr. Baker thinks…"

"No, no. There's no need for that. You have been making wonderful strides, but there's no need to push too fast."

I meet his eyes.

"So, you'll go?"

"Anything for you, Darling."

I smile at him and lean in for a kiss. My body slides off the arm of the chair and into his lap, letting me press my hand to his chest. His eyes drift closed, and his mouth opens. I let his tongue venture between my lips and his hands pull me closer. It makes it easier for my hands to rove over his chest and slide under the sides of his jacket. As his tongue dips into my mouth, my fingers dip into the little pocket and draw out the key. It folds into my palm, and I continue the kiss just long enough to keep his mind fogged.

"Thank you." I hop off his lap and turn around quickly, so he won't notice the key go into the fold of my belt. "I'll make you a list."

I jot down the ingredients I need and hand them to him before excusing myself to the restroom. The key goes under a metal canister of cleanser in the cabinet under the bathroom sink before I come back out. It's too risky to keep carrying it around.

"Let me call the order in," he says. "I'll have the store get everything ready for us."

It's something he's done before, and the concept of it fascinates me. I wonder who he's actually calling when he picks up the kitchen phone and where he actually gets the groceries.

We sit down at the table for the early supper I've prepared. He talks as he eats, but my mind is on nothing but that key and the locked drawer in his study. When he's finished, Charles sets out to pick up chocolate and peppermint, and I set myself in front of a sealed kitchen window to do the dishes. I count the seconds after he walks out of the house. Him ordering the groceries means I have far less time. I won't be able to search as much as I wanted to, but it will give me a glimpse.

The lock releases under the key, and I rush to the desk. A harsh sound from the drawer opening makes the hair on the back of my neck stand up. I stop, holding my position, waiting for something to happen. It doesn't, and I reach into the drawer for the first file, opening it on the desk.

"Mallory Maynard," I whisper. "Unattached. Very accessible." I turn the page. "Challenging personality. Uncooperative and combative. Will not listen to reason. Easily embarrassed and unwilling to try to connect. Has never cooked and will not try. Smashed two windows." I nod. "Good for her."

The name sounds so familiar, but I can't place it. I read it again and again, trying to figure out where I've heard it before. I want to keep reading, but I can't risk taking too much time. Everything needs to be back in place and the dishes done by the time Charles gets home.

With any luck, I can jump right in to making the fudge, and he will go to bed before trying to lure me with him.

I tuck the folder back into the drawer and reluctantly lock it. The key goes back under the metal canister, and I rush back to the kitchen to continue the dishes. He'll expect the dishes to be done when he gets home. After all, there's nothing else for me to do but make sure the house stays perfect. I go through them as fast as I can and am placing the last serving dish in the cabinet when Charles walks back into the house.

"That was fast," I tell him.

He has a slightly odd expression in his eyes when he comes into the kitchen. They trace over me and the empty sink, then my hand as I slide it back over my head to smooth my hair.

"They had everything you need," he smiles, holding a bag out to me.

I smile and rise up on the balls of my feet to reward him with a kiss to the cheek before taking the bag. I bring it over to the pink Formica kitchen table and start unloading the ingredients. Some of the labels look odd, companies I've never heard of, but I know why. Attention to detail. Custom crafted labels and collectibles to ensure the correct year. The thought makes my skin cold.

"Thank you. This is perfect."

His favorite word. His lullaby.

"You haven't told me what you're making," he says, stepping up beside me and running his hand down along my back.

"Peppermint fudge," I tell him. "Don't you recognize the ingredients? I make it every Christmas."

He looks down at the table and then back at me. A question flickers across his eyes, and he replaces it with a smile.

"I suppose I've never paid attention to the ingredients. I'm just interested in the finished fudge."

My giggle is masterful, the effect immediate. All the tension slides out of him.

"There will be plenty for you." I let out a soft sigh. "This makes me miss Vivian."

"Vivian?" he asks.

I slide my eyes over to him.

"My sister. She shared this recipe with me so many years ago. We used to make it together every year before she got married and moved away. Some of my favorite Christmas memories are making up a big batch of this fudge to give to friends and neighbors and sitting at the kitchen table writing cards while we wait for the chocolate to melt."

"You remember that?" he asks.

His voice starts low, but lifts at the end, like he realized the tone and caught the sagging words to toss them back up into a question steeped in excitement.

"I do, thanks to you. I was so confused by what I was seeing when I was filling out the cards last week, but you reminded me of Vivian, and it became so clear. She's so beautiful. I hope we'll be able to travel out to see her next year for Christmas."

"Oh?" Charles asks.

I nod and move around the kitchen taking out bowls and pots to start the fudge so it can be ready tomorrow morning.

"With Dr. Baker's help, and you, Dear, I know I can overcome these challenges. We can really start living our lives. Our *life*. Together. And that would be the most amazing trip. She lives all the way across the country – we could go to Disneyland. By then it will be even more magnificent. So much can happen in a year and a half of being open."

Charles takes me into his arms and touches a soft kiss to my lips. I taste tears in them, and I wonder if I might have taken a step too far.

CHAPTER TWENTY-ONE

NICK

Matilda hadn't heard anything, but she didn't have the reaction Nick thought she would. Rather than her panic getting stronger and her agreeing to come join him in searching for her daughter, she had gotten more suspicious. There was a note in her voice every time they spoke that said she was just waiting for Nick to admit he had done something to her. But he couldn't stop reaching out to her. It didn't matter what she thought. He knew the truth, and it was going to take everyone possible to search for her.

The police wouldn't listen when he called them again and said he thought he knew who took his wife, not even when he said it was possible she was already dead. Not even when he said he had followed Alex to the edge of the woods and seen him disappear down a narrow road that led to nowhere and was far from his home.

It was like they didn't even hear him. Just a man whose wife left him. A man who needed to recognize what he had done to drive her away and either accept that she was gone or find a way to get her back. Nick would never accept that she was gone. Even if it took until his last breath, he would find her. No matter what Alex did to her, he would bring her home.

Then he would deal with Alex.

The doorbell ringing was startling in the quiet house. Nick wasn't expecting anyone to come by, but he especially wasn't expecting the face he saw through the glass beside the door. He walked past the foyer table in bare feet. There was no more glass to dig into his skin, and the cold had been chased away by the fire he kept burning in the fireplace every moment he was home. Watching the flames dance comforted him.

Alex leaned to the side to look through the glass and grinned at him, waving cheerfully. Nick wrenched open the door and glared out at him.

"Hello, Mr. Whitman," he said.

"Merry Christmas, Helmsworth. Please, call me Alex. I think we've been working together long enough for that. Especially if you are going after that promotion. I have it in good authority you are in the running."

He laughed, and Nick managed a lukewarm smile.

"Alex."

"That's better. And I guess that means I'll call you Nick. Sounds appropriate. 'Tis the season, after all."

That was really enough of that. Nick had gotten his fill of the cheery holiday small talk, especially with him. His hands ached to wrap around Alex's neck and throttle him, but he couldn't. Not until he found Liza and knew everything this man had done to her.

"Is there something I can do for you?" Nick asked.

Alex produced a Christmas-themed tin wrapped in a red satin bow.

"I brought you something."

Nick was torn between his hatred of Alex and his manners. Desire to pull any information about Liza out of him overrode both of them. He stepped to the side and gestured with one arm to the entryway.

"Would you like to come in?" he asked.

There was no sincerity in his voice, but Alex seemed to create all of it he needed and smiled enthusiastically.

"Absolutely."

"This way."

They walked into the house, and Nick led him into the living room. Alex looked around and then turned his smile to Nick.

"You know, I believe this is the first time I've been to your home."

"I think so."

He pointed to a wedding picture hanging on the wall. Nick had taken it down in the first days after Liza left, but it returned to its spot a few days ago. Stinging grey eyes fell on Liza just like they did when Alex sat at the end of the dock and stared at his phone.

"And this is your wife?"

Nick rolled his neck, trying to keep himself calm.

"Yes," he said through gritted teeth.

Alex turned to him with an apologetic look on his face.

"I'm sorry," he said. "I didn't think before I spoke."

Nick shook his head.

"It's true," he said. "That is my wife. Liza is still my wife; she just isn't here."

Their eyes met. Alex searched his face for a few moments before the smile slid back into place. He held the tin out to Nick.

"This is compliments of Mrs. Whitman," he said. "She sends her regrets that you weren't able to attend the party and wants you to know you are appreciated. By both of us. It's her sister's recipe."

The tin felt heavy as Alex handed it over, but it didn't seem to have to do with what was in it. The words hung around them.

"Thank you," Nick said.

Alex nodded and let out an awkward sigh. He glanced around like he was waiting for something else, then started toward the door.

"Well, I'll be going. Have a wonderful holiday. I look forward to seeing you in January."

It sounded like the outgoing message on a corporate voicemail account. Nick followed him to the door.

"You, too," he said. "Thanks for stopping by."

He shut the door behind Alex before he could give in to his compulsion to follow him. Not right now. It would be too obvious. He took a step back from the door and was headed back toward the living room when he realized he was still holding the tin. The red ribbon held a card on top, and Nick slid it out of place. He opened it and saw an obviously photoshopped picture of Alex and a dark-haired woman posing in front of a fireplace.

Happy holidays to you and yours. The Whitmans

Tossing the card onto the entryway table, Nick set down the tin and used his fingers to pry the lid out of place. He didn't even need to see what was beneath the pieces of delicate tissue paper for his heart to start pounding in his chest; the smell was enough. But he moved the paper aside anyway. As soon as he saw the fudge, the lid dropped from his hand, and he ran to the living room where he dug through the only box of Christmas items he hadn't fully obliterated. A moment later, he stuffed his feet into shoes without bothering to put socks on, grabbed his coat, and flew out the door.

Mrs. Whitman's sister's recipe, my ass.

He grabbed his phone as his car skidded around the corner out of his neighborhood.

"I need to speak to Detective Jefferson about a missing persons report," he said when a man obviously exasperated to be working answered the phone. "I have new information about the disappearance of my wife. I believe I know where she is and that she is in serious danger." He turned onto the next road and saw Alex's car ahead of him, he honked the horn and gestured for Alex to pull into the next parking lot. "Her name is Mary Elizabeth Helmsworth. Liza."

———

Mary/Liza

As soon as Charles walks back inside, I'm focused on the shimmering silver envelope in his hand. Even from this distance I know it is smooth and heavy, cardstock sprinkled with tiny embossed snowflakes.

"What's that?" I ask.

Charles looks at the envelope as if he's forgotten he was holding it.

"Oh, this is from one of my employees," he says. "He was very appreciative of the fudge."

"Oh?"

He forces a hint of a laugh.

"He was so touched, he even forgot to give me the card when I was at his house. He chased me down after I left."

I laugh and reach for it.

"That's very sweet. May I see it?"

Charles hands it to me, and I feel a ripple of current rush through me as soon as my fingertips touch the paper. I don't show what I'm feeling as my fingers slip beneath the flap on the envelope, releasing the adhesive. My skin searches for the lingering remnants of him, of the tongue that touched the seal, the laugh that sounds like rain, and the kiss that feels like sun on my face. Pulling the card carefully from the envelope, I open it and look at handwriting that brings tears to my eyes.

"What does it say, Darling?" Charles asks.

"May your holiday season be as warm as a fire in a home with no heat and as sweet as carrot cake."

I can barely control the tremble in my voice, and my eyes struggle to hold back tears.

"That's a strange inscription," he frowns. "But I suppose he is a particular type of fellow."

"Who is?" I make myself ask. "There's no signature."

To prove my point, I turn the card around and show Charles the blank space beneath the message. He looks at me, and I stare plainly into his eyes, not flinching. It isn't hard to look into his eyes and lie. I've been doing it without knowing for six months. No one would ever have to tell me this card is from Nick. Christmas will always bring to mind the memory of the first one we spent together when we were dating. We wanted to make it special, and he invited me to stay at his parents' house while they were away visiting family. It took only two hours of a storm to knock the power out and one shared piece of carrot cake huddled in front of the fireplace that night to prove he is the love of my life.

Charles looks satisfied by the question and smiles.

"A cameraman named Nick."

"Just a cameraman?"

"He has designs on being more, but he hasn't proven himself."

The words to defend Nick, *my husband,* bubble up inside my throat, but I force them down. Charles takes the card from my hand and brings it into the living room to display on the mantle. I notice him glancing around at his feet and around the furniture as he comes back into the kitchen.

"Is something wrong?" I ask.

"Have you seen my key?"

My stomach drops, the joy of feeling Nick so close to me, even if only through paper, drains out through my feet.

"Your key?"

I try to sound as casual as possible as I fall into my routine, putting out lunch, and making plans for supper.

"The key to my study. I can't find it."

"It's not in your jacket pocket?"

"If it was, I wouldn't be looking for it, Darling."

"I'm sorry. That is the only place I've ever known it to be."

My simpering makes him feel bad, and Charles comes to touch a kiss to the top of my head.

"It's alright, Darling. I'm sorry. I shouldn't have snapped at you."

"Have you seen it since you went to the property you bought?" I ask. "Could you have dropped it there?"

"I thought I had it after that." He felt his pockets again. "It wasn't in the laundry?"

I giggle for good measure.

"Your suits don't go into the washing machine, Dear."

Charles nods.

"That was silly of me. Maybe you're right. I know I have been away so much lately, but would you mind terribly if I went and looked for it? It's the only key I have, and I wouldn't want to have to call a locksmith this close to Christmas."

"Of course, I don't mind. You know what's best. I wouldn't want to bother a locksmith now, either," I tell him. "Sit down and have lunch, and then you can go."

Charles shakes his head.

"No. Please pack it up for me. I'll take it to eat in the car."

I don't argue. Less than five minutes, later he has a sack of sandwiches and potato chips in his hand and is heading out of the house with a cursory kiss to my cheek. Waiting is almost impossible. It's always hard to be patient when Charles leaves, but today I feel myself twitching, shaking with anticipation. Finally, I can't wait any longer. I run down the hallway to the study and go straight for the desk, gathering out all the folders in the locked drawer. Then I rush to the guest room to reclaim what's really mine.

I shouldn't pause. I shouldn't take a single second longer. But I can't resist the suitcase full of my clothes. Low pumps get kicked across the room. Dress, crinolines, and petticoats fall to the ground. Lingerie drops to the discarded pile of fabric. In their place, my own bra and panties. My own jeans. My own t-shirt. My own sweatshirt. I'm trying to stuff everything into my bag when I hear the sound I so desperately didn't want to hear.

The front door slamming.

CHAPTER TWENTY-TWO

NICK

The soundstage loomed ahead of him as Nick pounded down the paved path toward it. Alex was nowhere in sight, but he knew this was the place. The massive nondescript cement building sat in a clearing. It looked fairly small from that angle, taking up the equivalent of a few city blocks, but it stretched endlessly into the distance, covering acres. On the sides he could see, the soundstage was surrounded by a variety of large trees whose branches reached out like fingers, grasping at the sun.

His breath was shallow and forced as he forced his legs to churn toward the door in the distance. He slowed as he reached it, skidding to a halt by ramming his body into the metal door. Trying to turn the knob did nothing. He yanked on it, hoping for any movement at all.

A roar of panic and rage came from deep within his chest, and his hands slipped off the knob. In frustration, he kicked the door, hoping against hope that he could dent it, move it, just slightly. Enough to get his fingers in. He had to find a way in. The door didn't budge, and it didn't dent. It stood as it was, the only evidence of his kick a slight smudge from the rubber of his shoe. There had to be another way in. Something. Anything.

His head whipped around as he surveyed the area around him,

hoping for a crowbar or a pipe or even a large branch. Something he could swing at the door, or any other opening. Nothing. The area around the building was empty but for flowers. It looked manicured. Fake.

Something glinted in the flowerbed. He ran to it, hoping what he was seeing was real. It was almost around on the other side of the building, but the setting sun shone on it like a beacon of hope. He darted for it, mind racing as to how to use it. As his hands clasped around the wooden handle, the plan formed in his mind. It wouldn't work. He knew it wouldn't. But he had to try. Running back to the door with the shovel in hand, he aimed it at the small empty space between the door and the frame.

Nick jammed the shovel point end first, into the crack. It stuck, and he shoved it down, smashing into the silver lock. It didn't give. He tried again, pushing all his weight into it, and again, it just clanged against the lock and refused to budge. He tried to wedge it, inching it down, but nothing moved. Beads of sweat collected on his eyebrows, and he had to wipe them away with his arm as he gripped the shovel tighter. Putting a foot on the doorframe he leaned back, pulling the shovel toward him until a snapping sound preceded him falling backwards onto the ground.

He tossed the now useless chunk of the shovel handle to the side and scrambled to his feet. The door wasn't going to open. He had to find another way in. Searching upward for a window or a ledge to climb, he saw a gap in the cement high in the air. He stepped back to get a better look and saw it was a vent, allowing air to escape the building, but not offering much in the way of an entrance.

"Come on," he muttered to himself.

Nick had to get inside the building. It was a massive, sprawling building, but he knew Liza was in there somewhere. Stepping away from the front door, he wandered around the building, noting the curious lack of a fire exit in the back, or anything other than the large ventilation shafts that stuck out at seemingly random places along the building, far too high to climb up to.

One of the shafts stuck out of the left side of the building, touching the branches of an outcrop of trees that had stretched their wandering fingers all the way over the trampled down walkway and reached the building itself. A few of them were just above the shaft, maybe two or three feet. Enough that if he could just get on that branch, he might have a chance.

He scolded himself as he tried to climb the tree. This was ridiculous. There was no way he could make it, but at the same time, he had to try. Climbing the tree was more difficult than he remembered from his childhood, back when swinging from branch to branch had been a game, when the risk of horrible injuries or death was just another aspect of the fun. Now his mind raced with what-if scenarios of him being stuck here, crumpled in a heap by the building, his neck snapped in two. They would never know why. Alex would make sure of that.

They would never find Liza.

He found purchase for his footing on a limb that had looked so solid from far away, and now looked so thin and brittle. One experimental step seemed to send the entire tree bending forward. There was no turning back now, though, and finding a branch to hold on to above him, Nick began to sidle his way across. He tried not to look down, to keep his mind focused on why he was doing this. He had to get to her, and if he could just get inside the building…

He was feet away from the building when his heart sank. Closer to the vents now, he could see that they weren't as large as they looked from the ground either. And they were grated, with steel bars closing the entrance to them, and soldered into place. Even if he could reach it, he wouldn't be able to get in.

He took a moment to try to think, and a sound behind him forced him out of it. It was the cracking of a branch. He couldn't tell for sure if it was his, but he couldn't take the chance. He began to inch his way back, not wanting to rock it too much. Closer now, he could see where the wood was split, and as the tip of his shoe reached the sturdier part of the tree, it snapped.

The blinding rage stopped the pain when his body hit the ground. He scrambled to his feet and took a step back to look at the building again. He couldn't get inside. All entrances in this section were tightly closed, and there was no guarantee even if he did run down to the opposite end of the building, fighting through the acres of trees, that there would be another entrance he could use. He would waste all that time. Time Liza might not have. There had to be another way. Something that would get Alex away from Liza and give Nick the time to find her.

In an instant, he took off running toward the car he'd left parked out of sight so he could approach quietly on foot. There was only one thing that might draw Alex away from the soundstage. It was time for The Boss to get back to work.

CHAPTER TWENTY-THREE

ALEX

He had the key to his study when he came home from showing Nick the contract for the camp. He knew he did. He could remember walking into the house and going into the study to leave his briefcase. Suspicion burned in his chest, but Alex tried to stop it from becoming anger. There had to be an explanation.

He hadn't been gone from the house long before he turned the car around and headed back. The key had to be somewhere in the house. There was no other place that could be. He walked into the house and immediately felt something off. Something changed in the atmosphere. It no longer felt like home. He could hear something rustling down the hallway, and he headed down it toward the nursery. The door stood open, and the flicker of anger started to swell and build. Mary was in the nursery, doing something far more than dusting.

The first thing he saw when he stepped up to the door was her dress crumpled in the middle of the floor. Pink with small white dots, it was one of his favorites. Angela had been particularly proud of that one when he'd gone into the vintage store that he purchased clothes for Mary from. He wanted the house to be ready for her when he welcomed his new wife, and that dress had been what he looked forward to seeing her in the most.

Mary was standing in front of the door to the closet. It was closed, but she was far too close to it to be a coincidence.

"What are you doing?" Alex asked.

His eyes burned with fury as they took in the clothes she was wearing. They disgusted him. It was things like that in the pictures Nick showed that made him know she needed him. No woman as beautiful as Mary should be dressing in clothes like that. Yet, there she stood in front of him, the lovely dress he bought for her thrown on the ground and her choosing to wear veritable rags instead. Something in her hand caught his attention. It was a metallic glint she tried to twist into her palm and conceal, but she couldn't.

Alex stepped forward and grabbed her wrist. Mary tried to pull back from him, but he held tight. His other hand dug into her closed fist to wrench open her fingers and snatch back the key to his study. She stood her ground defiantly.

"Your name is Alex," she said slowly, her voice dark. "Alex Whitman, not Charles."

"My name is Charles Alexander Whitman," Alex told her. "Charles to you."

"Why?"

"Alex is only for when I am at work."

"With my husband."

The back of his hand cracked against her cheekbone. Mary stumbled. In that moment, she was nothing but Liza. Common, unpolished, forgettable.

"Don't you dare speak to me that way."

She straightened and met his eyes.

"You are Alex Whitman. You own a production company where you work with Nick Helmsworth. My husband."

She lifted her chin without flinching when he took a step toward her. Alex let his fingertips trace down her cheek and along her jawline.

"I saved you," he whispered.

"And Rebecca? I don't have a sister, Alex. I never have. The blonde woman I remembered, that was Rebecca."

"An unfortunate incident."

Mary... Liza... scoffed.

"An unfortunate incident? You killed her."

She started inching her way to the side, moving toward the door. Alex followed.

"Why would you say such a thing?" he asked. "I know how hard you work to keep that kitchen clean. You always have. Ever since we were married."

"We aren't married, Alex. I've only been here for six months."

"Don't be silly. We've been married for years. The blonde woman was your sister, Vivian."

"I don't have a sister," she said again, moving closer to the door. "That was Rebecca. She was here when I came. You wanted both of us. Then something happened, and you wanted to get rid of her. So, you did. You murdered her in the kitchen and almost killed me in the process, then dragged both of us outside. I watched you bury her. That's when I lost my memory."

"You don't know what you're saying," Alex said, trying to reason with her.

This was going to be more difficult than he hoped. But he had been through it before. He knew how to mold her. He would start again if he had to.

"Yes, I do."

He lunged to stop her from getting to the door, but she dodged him, scrambling around him and running. Alex chased after her and grabbed hold of the back of her sweatshirt, yanking her back against him.

"Why are you being like this?" he asked. "Come on, Darling. We are so happy. Why do you want to ruin our happiness?"

"I don't even know you," she hissed.

His hand was sliding up the center of her chest toward her throat when the phone in his study rang. Any time he was home, calls to his cell phone were redirected to that phone. It could be anyone. He growled and yanked her with him to the door to the study. Using the key he had just taken back from her, Alex unlocked the door and dragged her with him to the desk.

"Yes?" he barked.

"Mr. Whitman?"

"Yes. Who is this?"

He usually had better phone manners, but in this situation, he had other things on his mind.

"This is the River View Fire Department. We received a call reporting a fire at a property listed in your name. The Camp Pine Trails."

Alex bit off the profanity that tried to make its way out of his mouth.

"I'll be right there."

He slammed the phone down and pulled Mary back out of the study, locking it and firmly stuffing the key into his pocket. He brought her to the bedroom and shoved her down onto the bed.

"Don't move," he warned and stomped out of the house.

Liza

There is more fear in my veins than blood. But as soon as Alex leaves the house, I jump up from the bed and run for the guest room again. I finish packing and go to the front door; hopeful his rush means he didn't lock it. My hope is instantly dashed. I am trying to think of the next option for how to get out of the house when the phone rings.

Not the phone in Alex's study, but the pink one in the kitchen. It's attached to the wall beside the refrigerator, and I have never touched it. Too anxious, Alex always told me. Too afraid to speak to strangers. He never called me, and I didn't know anyone else, so there was never a reason to touch the receiver. This is the first time I've heard its tone.

I tremble as I walk up to it and lift the receiver.

"Hello?"

"Turn on the TV, Mary," Alex says in a slick, almost flirtatious tone. "There's someone who wants to talk to you."

The cord is long enough for me to bring it with me into the living room. I turn the dial on the television. My mind expects *I Love Lucy* or *The Honeymooners*. Instead, I see Alex's face. He's outside, standing on sandy ground.

"What are you doing?" I ask into the phone.

He steps to the side, and I see Nick on the ground, his hands and feet bound, blood trickling from his nose.

CHAPTER TWENTY-FOUR

ALEX

"Hello, Liza," Alex said, his voice slithering like an eel as he marveled at himself.

He heard the phone receiver fall to the floor and ended the call on his own phone. He opened an app and pressed a button, then tucked the phone away in his pocket.

For once, she was going to see all the trouble he went to for her. For once, she would finally see how much he loved her.

"Sorry to interrupt your regularly scheduled soap opera, but I think Nick here has something to say, don't you?"

Walking into frame, Alex stood with an antique microphone, its sleek metal shell still emblazoned with the call letters of the station that had used it for newscasts before it was discarded and then found at a thrift shop so many years ago. Now he pointed the microphone at Nick, who struggled against the ropes. A muffled sound of rage came from deep within his chest against the tape across his mouth.

"No? Oh, I guess Nick is a little too tied up to speak now."

He laughed. It was the first time he had truly laughed in ages. It came from deep in his belly and spilled out of him in staccato bursts of baritone. For so long, he had laughed so meticulously, so measured. Like a Ward Cleaver laugh. A laugh that still had an air of authority, of control. A laugh that could be doled out for the right moment where it was needed. But this, this was a full-on Dick Van Dyke laugh. It was deep, booming, and sharp. He laughed until his belly hurt, and his eyes watered.

When the laughter had descended into a mild chuckle, he regained his composure and stared back at the camera. He had his usual audience of one, the woman who would be Perfect. If she only tried.

"Did you ever find the box on the back of the television, Liza? I'm sure you did. You must have cleaned the top of the set a thousand times, dusting away, and away. But did you ever pay attention to the little box with the blinking light? Didn't that ring a bell, Liza? Do you know what it was, Nick? Oh, you will love this. It was..." he mimicked a drum roll in the air.

Nick struggled in vain to get out of the ropes that held him so tightly, but they wouldn't budge. Alex had gotten very good with ropes over the years.

"It was a router, Liza! A router to connect to the internet. All this time, I have been streaming a channel I created online. I spent *days*, Liza. I spent days finding every episode in that TV guide and putting them on this channel. It was so much work. So very much work. I had to program the television to send a signal to change to another channel on the web. It took months to curate all of it. And the commercials! My goodness, Liza, you wouldn't believe how long it took to track down all those commercials."

There had been weeks spent finding all those shows, then days and days of creating the exact right stream for her to watch. Favors had been called in from studios so he could raid their archives. Thousands of dollars had been spent blindly buying reels at auction. Every single second of six months' worth of programming he had done by hand. Just for her. He had gone through so much just so she could change the dial on the set and see three different channels, exactly as the guide had said they would be. It had been perfect. Just for her.

Nick thrashed on the ground beside him, and Alex gave him a sharp kick in the hip to quiet him.

"But I would do it all again, Darling. I would do anything for you.

I already have. Only I didn't know it was for you. Not at first. I thought it was for someone else. I met her when I was just a boy. We went to summer camp together. She was so beautiful, so different from all the other girls. I knew then there was something special about her and decided she would be mine one day. But she never noticed me." Alex shook his head slightly. "I couldn't really blame her. Everyone was charmed by her, enchanted by even a glance from her. She didn't know that. To her, it was her best friend who had everyone's attention. But I knew the truth. I saw her for what she really was. She was everything, and I was just the boy who went to private schools during the year and then had his rich parents dump him off at the camp so they could travel through Europe in the summers. I hadn't proven myself yet. I wasn't deserving of her attention."

Alex shook his head, taking a step closer so Liza would see the sincerity in his eyes.

"Don't let that bother you, Darling. I didn't know you then. I was blinded by her. Every year I looked forward to seeing her, and every summer, I worked toward gaining her attention. A few times, she spoke to me, but it never went beyond that. As we got older, her friends became cruel. They were brutal toward me and ensured I never got close to her. I had to watch as she dedicated herself to boys who could never please her and then to a best friend who treated her like a puppet."

"You," Nick growled, having pulled his mouth free from the tape. "You and your fucking movie. That was it the whole time. You just wanted to get your hands on Lisanne."

Alex looked down at him. Hearing him speak was infuriating, but at least he understood.

"It was brilliant, don't you think? I could craft my own reality. That's what my father always taught me. In the movies, anything is possible. You can escape from the cold cruelty of the world into a beautiful fantasy. Anything you want, anything you can possibly dream of, can be yours. That's what I would do. For me and for her. I'd save her from a world that wasn't good enough for her and show her what life could truly be. A lovely home, a devoted husband, a world where she doesn't have to worry about anything."

"Where she can be a puppet," Nick snapped.

Alex shoved him with his foot again.

"Not a puppet. A *wife*. My wife. We'd leave now and go to 1955. I have always thought the world was at its best then and in the few years after. We could reset our existence and relive the peace, comfort, and prosperity. Everything would be as it should be. But I had learned. I'd learned from many years of trying to earn her heart that I couldn't just jump into it. No." He shook his head, staring into the lens of the camera and envisioning Liza staring into his eyes. "I had to be ready. Really ready. I had to practice and ensure I could be the very best husband I could be. Unfortunately, that took some sacrifice, but it was necessary. It was what had to be done. Everything was falling into place exactly the way it was supposed to. I'd make a movie to commemorate the fifteenth anniversary of the last summer we spent at camp, the summer Bethany DeAngelis disappeared. We'd bring in original campers. Lisanne would be there. She would finally see me. Then everything changed.

Alex crouched down so he could be close to Nick's face.

"You see, Nicholas here had begun to show off pictures of his lovely wife. So sweet. So beautiful. But so mishandled. I knew as soon as I saw you, he couldn't be the right husband for you. A lowly laborer barely bringing in enough money to support a bachelor properly. I should know. I'm the one who paid him. You deserved so much more. At the time, I felt sad for you. My eyes were still set on Lisanne, and I could only hope you would one day find the one who could give you the life you deserve. But then I thought... why? Why should sweet Liza be forced to suffer a classless brute of a husband when I have more than enough love and devotion for two perfect women?"

He rubbed his chin with one hand. A buzzing sound was growing in his ears, and it felt like the ground was starting to get uneven beneath his feet. The rush of those summer weeks was coming back to him. He felt the adrenaline tinging his blood and pounding in his

CHAPTER TWENTY-FIVE

LIZA

There is a sudden sound sharp metallic sound, like a hundred prison cells being slammed shut at once. It comes from everywhere. My heart jumps in my chest, and my head whips around, trying to find the sound. I've sunk down to the ground as I watched Alex talk on the screen, and I hunch closer to it, trying to protect myself against whatever I'm hearing.

Alex has disappeared from the screen, leaving it with nothing but gray and white interference. Snow. Suddenly I know what the sound is. Locks. The front door secures itself beyond the three keyed locks; thick boards snap down over the windows, there is even an echo of the remote-activated locks coming from below me, as if the floor itself just locked itself tight. I have nowhere to go. I can't escape. And Nick is going to die.

No. I can't let that happen. Alex has taken everything from me for six months. He took me from my home, my husband, and my life. He tried to mold me into this Norman Rockwell wife without my permission. And he just expects me to deal with it, to change and become his perfect wife.

I have to find a way out.

I begin running through the house. There is a limited time before he will get here, and I need to find something to help me. My first thought is the kitchen phone. I have avoided using it all this time because the only person I ever talked to was Alex. I could kick myself for not using it before. I could have called anyone, any time. My stomach sinks as it occurs to me; I didn't know anyone's number until two days ago. I run over to it now, various numbers running through my head as to who to call first. By the time I reach it, I decide that 9-1-1 should be first. Then, if there's time, someone else.

I yank the receiver off the base and shove it to my ear so hard that the base falls off the wall, hanging by its cord. Nothing. No dial tone. No operator. No click sounds. Nothing at all. I wiggle the cord in the hopes I had just pulled too hard, but there is nothing still. He disconnected the phone. I throw it down, my hands automatically going to the sides of my head, like I am trying to push my head on either side to force it to think. I spin around, looking around the room for anything I can use.

It hits me. The phone in the study. The one on Alex's desk he would use to talk when he didn't want me listening. It was an old, ornate one, with gold on the receiver and mouthpiece and wood handles and ivory numbers. It was beautiful, and yet it always made me feel uneasy to see him pick it up. Like it shouldn't work.

I begin to cross the room to the study when the lights go out. It is so sudden and disorienting that I trip over myself and crash hard into the dining room table. My elbow is badly bruised, and I roll my ankle, but I have to get up. I have to find a way out of here and get help. I begin to feel my way through the room, walking by memory through tables and chairs arranged on hardwood floors that I had dusted and mopped and scrubbed so many times. I always kept it so neat, and yet, every day I had spent scrubbing something, as if it ever really got dirty. It was like I had been trying to scrub away the facade of what I couldn't make feel like my real life. If I just used a bit more polish, the floor would gleam back at me, and I'd see my real face.

I am steps away from the door when the lights flash back on again.

It is blinding, and white, and my eyes close, and my hand goes in front of my face instinctively. I crumple to the ground, trying to orient myself again. He is doing this. He is cutting the lights on and off to distract me, to mess with me. To control me.

I stand up again, closing my eyes against the brightness and fumbling my way to the doorknob. I know it will be locked, but I have to try. Just in case. My hand closes on it, and the lights go out again at the same time. I open them now, preparing to shut them again if they snap back on. I can make out vague shadows beyond the spots in my vision. The door is locked. I put my shoulder into the door, hoping that it might not be latched all the way, but it does nothing. Smashing my shoes into the solid wood is useless. I'm just wasting time and energy.

I try to think of anything else. There's the crawlspace, but there's no way of knowing if it actually leads anywhere. And he could lock me in. I can't hide in the bedroom or the bathroom because he would find me too easily. The house has no clutter, nothing to hide behind or under. Everything is in its place, and it all has enough space to see the floor underneath, so I have plenty of room to clean it. I have to find a way to surprise him or to run out of the door while he is inside.

There is nothing. The only thing I can think of is the study. The phone. The one line to the outside world that I am sure he would never disconnect. His line.

I take a few steps back to get a running start when the lights flash on again. This time they go on and off in a pattern. I shield my eyes and wait. Soon they click off again, and I dart for the door, crouching low and smashing into it as close to the handle as I can with all of my body weight. It creaks. It isn't exactly breaking down, but it's a start. My shoulder hurts, but I don't care. I have to get help before he kills Nick. I've seen what he does to people who don't fit in his perfect narrative. Nick will be first. I will be not long after that.

I ram into the door again, and I can hear wood starting to break. Unfortunately, my shoulder also feels like it's breaking. I know I can't keep hitting the door like this. I have to find something heavy I can

169

use. Fumbling in the darkness, I make my way over to a bookshelf. On the third row, all the way to the right. There it is. A small, but heavy, bust of Alfred Hitchcock. It is such a cliché I almost have to laugh. There'll be time for that later. I pull it off the shelf, knocking over a pair of binoculars that sit beside it, sending them bouncing across the floor beside me.

Feeling my way back, I stand in front of the door now, holding the bust in both hands. I raise it up and swing, aiming to hit just below the knob. As it lands, I can hear the wood creak again, and I know I am almost in. I slam it again and again. Each time, wooden pieces start to fall off the doorframe and the door itself. Each time putting more stress on the simple lock inside. Each time getting closer to inside the room. To the phone. To help.

I slam it again, and I think I hear something outside. Panic sets in, and I begin wailing on the door. Finally, there is a crack, and the bust goes through the door, creating a hole to the other side. It's small, but I might be able to reach my hand in and turn the lock. I stick my hand in, but it gets stuck, and I can't move. There is more sound from outside now, like doors slamming shut. The lights flick back on, and it takes a moment to adjust my eyes again. Tears are streaming down my face as I try to either shove my hand all the way through or pull it out.

"Darling," I hear.

The voice is coming from outside the door. He's playing with me. He thinks this is fun. A game.

I shove my hand one more time, and it breaks through to the other side. Reaching up, I fumble for the lock, and it opens. I pull my hand back out, and wood rips at my skin, cutting me open and sending droplets of shiny red blood all over the gleaming white door and the sparkling wooden floor. I whimper in pain but try to keep the sound from being too loud. I don't want him to know where I am. I have to think fast now because there is only one chance at this.

The key is in the door. I hear it catch. It opens, with the faintest of creaks. He had tried many times to keep the door from creaking, but it never would. There was always a sound. I was grateful for it because it was always the first sound to announce his arrival and the last sound before he left. It gave me warning, and it gave me relief.

He is standing in the doorway now. My vision is blocked, but I can just hear him and feel his presence. I tiptoe to my destination, not wanting to give away my hastily put together plan. Stepping lightly, I move fully out of sight and try to hold my breath. This has to work.

This has to work.

CHAPTER TWENTY-SIX

NICK

Water. Nick could smell water. Not ocean water with its saltiness, but lake water. Muddy and earthy and clean. Water made for late-night skinny dipping. He could hear it sloshing against... what exactly? Something surrounded him, encasing him, protecting him even. A splash of the water rose up and landed on his chin, rolling down the side of his cheek. That meant he was lying down.

He tried to open his eyes, but they wouldn't budge. Everything hurt. His arms were sore and bruised, pulled up and secured above his head. He tried moving them, but they barely shifted. His legs were the same, bound at the ankles, so he had a very little range of movement. It took a few moments to register the feeling of something on his wrists. Scratchy, like hay, or hemp or... rope. Rope. His hands were tied above his head. His legs, too. On either side of him, something hard rose several inches above his face. He was trapped inside of something. The rope brought back bitter memories, and Nick fought to stay calm.

Forcing his eyes open, he could see stars, trillions of them it seemed, sparkling in an inky-blue darkness. His head pounded, and his ribs ached, but his brain instantly tried to find the Big Dipper.

That was always her favorite. Every time he searched the night sky, he looked for it, for her. She wasn't there.

She was trapped.

Everything came rushing back. His Liza, trapped. Alex tying him up and hitting him. The beating that came after the camera was off. The feeling of helplessness that he couldn't save his wife. He hoped she had run. If she ran, she might find someone to help her. Maybe she was safe somewhere, wrapped in a blanket with a cup of coffee in her hand, a policeman asking her questions. Maybe there was hope. Maybe they would send a crew out here and find him, trapped inside this... whatever it was he was in. It shifted under him, and suddenly he knew. He was tied in a canoe. The chill rushed over him. Hope faded.

His mind filled with thoughts of her. For so long, he had thought she had left him, that she hated him, despised him, and the life they had built together. For so long, he had hated himself for losing her. Every breath he took in his waking hours, a little voice in the back of his mind had muttered all the worst things about himself that he believed, all spawned by the words on that note. But they weren't true, he told himself now. She never left me. She was taken.

That bastard had taken her.

Years he had worked with him, pored over scripts and sets and audition tapes. Late night take-out sessions and up-until-dawn rewrites. All the while, he was capable of doing this. Nick had listened as Alex laid it out for Liza, explaining how he had gotten her into his mind and chose her for his wife. His second wife. No, his... third. The number of women was dizzying. The thought of what might have happened to the two that came before her made bile rise in his throat.

Nick wondered if there was a sign he should have noticed. Alex was always a little odd, but in the film industry, that was relative. Words like 'passionate' and 'eccentric' were used to hide how absolutely creepy some people could be. Wiping away how 'off' they were by waxing poetic about the strangeness of genius and art. Most of the time, the weird ones really were harmless. They would invariably turn out to hate the crusts on sandwiches, or they had rituals that involved crystals, or they thought the Earth was flat. But Alex, he had seemed tame next to them, almost normal. He was a bit obsessive about things being 'period', but Nick had always chalked that up to dedication to realism. He was The Boss.

Now he knew better.

The canoe rocked. It wasn't the rock of a wave or a current, but the intentional rocking of a person. It rocked back and forth, harder each time until he felt it go up on its side. Nick could hear a grunt of effort as it turned all the way up and then came crashing back to the water. Just before the top of the canoe hit the surface of the water, he caught a glimpse of a man, his arms in the air, the sweat of physical effort rolling off his face. Nick knew him. The man with dishwater hair and empty eyes who followed Alex like a puppy in the hopes of getting cast in any role he could. Now, he'd been given a new task.

Suddenly Nick was submerged. The canoe bobbed down and then back up as the air trapped inside pulled it mostly above the surface. He was tied to the bottom of the inside, meaning he was now suspended above the water, which was beginning to leak in. He had been soaked when it went underwater, and the weather, which was already chilly, was now freezing on his wet clothes. He stared down into the blackness of the water, his breath catching as his body started to shiver. Pale wisps of his hot breath came from his nose as he tried to calm himself and breathe deeply.

It was so dark he could barely make out any light at all, but what was there only served to show the opening of the canoe and the water slowly filling it. Soon it would begin to sink, and as it did, so would he. He would drown, slowly, watching the water come and fill up his mouth, fill up his throat, fill up his lungs.

He had heard drowning wasn't so bad, that most people went unconscious before their lungs filled up and they died. He didn't know if he believed that. Maybe that was just something we tell ourselves, so we don't have to think of how terrified the person who died was. How horrible it is to know that you are dying and that there's nothing you can do. That the water will take you, just as it bore your ancestors millions of years ago.

175

Nick struggled against the ropes on his arms, but they had very little give. Maybe enough, he thought, to get one arm loose. If he could just get one arm loose. He had always been a decent swimmer, so if he could get out of the ropes, he had a chance. He yanked on the ropes on both wrists and found that they were pulling on each other. Pulling on both just made them tighter. He had to focus on one wrist and try to escape. There wasn't enough time for the police to save him, even counting for how long he must have been out. He had minutes before the canoe would capsize, and then it would be too late. He would be dead maybe a minute, two minutes later. He wondered how long he could hold his breath. How long would he have under the water before he had to let go.

Pulling on just one wrist seemed to create a little space. The rope was still tight around it, cutting into his skin and burning with every movement. But perhaps a little moisture would help, even blood. Something that would help create some space between him and the rope and let him slip out. Trying to turn his wrist in one direction and then the other, Nick tried frantically to escape. But the cold was getting to him. His body was bruised and beaten. Little droplets of blood were forming perfect circles in the water as they dropped off his forehead. Somewhere near his eyebrow, he was cut. The blood dripped off him like sweat as he kept pulling at the rope.

Stopping for a moment to catch his breath and rest his arm, he thought of Liza again. He wondered if she was still in that soundstage. He wondered if she would accept the new reality, even for a little while. Liza was a willful woman, but she was no actress. It was what he liked about her. She couldn't help but be herself all of the time. She wasn't capable of pretending to be someone else. Not on purpose.

But for the last six months, she had. Whether she realized it or not, she had been pretending, playing wife to Alex, doing what he told her to because that was her reality. For six months, she had been pretending to be the perfect housewife. And she had done it without even realizing she was doing it. There was so much more to experience with Liza, so much more to do. So many things left to learn about her. He couldn't just give up now. He had to fight. To stay alive. For her.

He exhaled deeply and began to wiggle his wrist again. He could see where it was pulled taut around a baseboard of the canoe. If he could rub the rope against it hard enough, and fast enough, maybe he could weaken it enough to snap it. He began to try, pulling it back and forth across the corner of the wood. But the rope seemed to be coated in something, some spray or material that made it strong and resistant to unraveling. His best bet was going to be getting a hand free.

He tried again, but nothing was moving. He had loosened it up as best he could already, and no amount of wiggling was going to get it open further. His wrist was now raw, and blood bubbled up in a few places where the rope had been. He waited for the bubbles to rise to the surface and then pulled hard, hoping that the blood would act as a slickening agent. His hand slid just a fraction of an inch further, but then stopped. It was something, but not enough.

A breeze blew across the lake and seemed to curl up in the canoe with Nick. He shuddered and turned his attention to his other wrist.

CHAPTER TWENTY-SEVEN

ALEX

"Honey," Alex said in a sing-songy voice, a smile stretching across his perfect teeth, "I'm home. I trust you had a wonderful day, my Darling," he said, loud enough that it should be heard and responded to.

When it wasn't, he stood stock-still, waiting. Of course, Mary would come to the door and greet him. Of course, she would take his coat and hat and kiss him on the cheek. Of course, she would forget all about that nasty business with Nick and have realized that she was exactly where she belonged now. She knew she was home. Surely.

She really had no choice.

He looked down at the smartphone in his hand. The app that allowed him to control the doors and lights was still up. He had fun turning them on and off. He could just imagine how powerful she must think he is, controlling the house from outside of it. And he was, too. A big powerful man. He could tell her in detail how strong he was, dragging that useless body all the way down to the lake. She would be so impressed, so enthralled. She would, of course, offer to rub his sore muscles. And, of course, that would lead to more. But not yet.

Right now, he had to make sure she understood. She was such a fragile little flower; he needed to make sure she knew just how much he loved her. Just how much he had *done* for her. Telling her about the television had been delicious. It must have blown her little mind to know how much work he had put into it, how long he had planned it, how much effort he had given before she even came to live with him.

He slipped the phone back into his briefcase. It was always on silent, as soon as he left work, but he kept it on, just in case he needed it. It had caused considerable difficulty in the last six months with producers and agents all wanting to get ahold of him at various times of the evening. He had taken to working long hours in the study, texting them back or telling them that he was off. He couldn't risk his lovely wife overhearing those conversations. They would just confuse her.

Stepping over the threshold, he noticed something was wrong. He could just see into the kitchen and noticed the phone, hanging off the wall, the cord exposed. That was so unlike her. The house was always kept neat as a pin, even impressing Alex himself, who was notoriously tidy. There was even a cup in the sink. It was positively jarring to see such wanton dereliction of her duties. He would have to have a stern talk with her later. Perhaps just before dinner. That way they could make up over dessert. He might even kiss her on the top of her head and tell her everything will be fine. Yes. That would be how he would handle it. A stern, guiding hand, followed by a comforting embrace. That was the order of things.

A step into the kitchen revealed more than he had ever feared. The table in the dining room was askew. A chair had been moved out of place. Further in, he could see his bookshelf in the living room. Books had fallen down on the third row, and his bust of Alfred Hitchcock must be on the floor somewhere. Perhaps she had been so shocked by what he had shown her on television she simply fell apart. That was the only possible explanation for such a terrible state.

Either that or she was testing him. Testing boundaries that she knew she should not test. Seeing where his temper lay. If so, he would have to show her exactly how much he cared for her by exerting his natural dominion over her as her husband. It wouldn't be pleasurable, not for her, and only a little for him. But it would be needed. She had to see that there was no room for that kind of rebellion. That kind of life only lead to chaos and worry and unseemliness. He wouldn't stand for that. She had been so close to the perfect wife up to now, and now she would truly be.

"Darling," he called out, in a tone that he hoped suggested worry and disappointment in one, "I see quite a mess. Are you not feeling well?"

It was giving her an out, he realized, but if she said that she was unwell, perhaps he could let it slide.

He was met with silence. A few steps further revealed a mess he had certainly not anticipated. His study door, which he locked with the app before heading back, was standing open. There was a hole in the door just below the knob, and blood streamed down from it.

"Darling," he said, his voice rising in both volume and concern, "you must be hurt. Come to me and let me help you."

More silence. Not even breathing. The buzzing in his ears and tingling on his skin was swelling again, taking over like it had beside the lake. She was hiding from him. How dare she?

Striding to the door, he swung it open. The room was as it always was, spotless. Except the phone. The ornate phone on his desk, the one with the separate line so he could speak to others without his wife listening in. The receiver was sitting on his desk, off the cradle. He walked up to it and hung it up.

She had touched his things. She had violated his trust and gone into his study, his one room of the home that was his alone, that he mostly kept up himself, his solitude, the place where he read, she had gone in there and *touched his things.* She had meddled. She had broken rules. She had disobeyed.

She was to be punished.

He took off out of the room, pounding his feet as he ran. It shook the house, but that was what he wanted. He wanted her to hear him coming. To fear the wrath of him. She had to know what she did was wrong, and that whatever was to become of her now was of her own doing.

He threw open the nursery door. It seemed empty, but there was always one place. Opening the closet door, he cringed when he saw the bent wallpaper and the open door. A fresh wave of disappointment and anger surged through him at the reminder of Mary's betrayal. He ducked down to look into it, expecting to find her cowering in the corner, adding herself to the remnants already.

The clothes, the jewelry, the pictures of the failures of before were still there. Nothing was gone, but she wasn't there.

Stomping away from the nursery, he began making his way for the bedroom. She might be there, waiting for him, ready to try to calm him down. She might even be in bed. He didn't know if that would work, but if she was going to try it, he would play along.

He opened the door to more silence. She wasn't there, he could tell. There was no space to hide in that room. He still ducked down to look under the dresser and behind the nightstand. He was about to call for her again when he heard a sound above him. In the attic.

Alex snuck down the hall, reaching up for the string that pulled open the trap door for the attic. How did she get up there and pull it closed? Sly little minx, she is. A little more of a handful now than she was before. That would have to change. Pulling down the steps carefully, so as to not make noise, he began to ascend to the attic.

It was cold up here without the benefit of the furnace pumping hot air into it and smelled like cardboard and unfinished wood and paint cans. He worked his way up the stairs until he was standing on the top step. Looking around, he saw nothing but shadows, but he swore he heard her up here. There weren't mice, or critters, not here. They never made it into this neighborhood. Turning his head, he looked for any movement, any change of light, listened for any sound.

"Darling, I need to speak with you," he said evenly, hoping to lure her out.

If he kept himself level, she wouldn't know how angry he was with her. If she would just confess and apologize, he wouldn't need to punish her too badly.

"Darling?" he asked. A sound from behind him made him turn. For a brief second, he saw the face of Alfred Hitchcock, and then nothingness.

CHAPTER TWENTY-EIGHT

NICK

Nick struggled against the rope again. It was useless. No matter how much fluid built up, water, sweat, blood, none of it was enough to get his wrist through. It was tied tight. He was trapped.

His body was shivering now, the cold seeping deep down into his bones. He couldn't tell if it was just because he was wet and cold, or if it was the loss of blood or a combination of both, but he knew he was starting to fade. So much energy was being wasted by shaking. So much breath being shot out of his lungs. Breath he would need, if for nothing else than to make his life last a few seconds longer.

But maybe not. Maybe he should just yell out and get all the air out before he sinks. Then take a big deep breath as soon as he was under. Go ahead. Get it all out of the way. Be done with it quickly. It had to be better than the slow suffering. It had to be easier. Faster. He wondered if it would count as a suicide then. If he would meet his maker and they would chide him for not fighting harder for his life.

Maybe. His life wasn't the one he was worried about, though. Liza's was. She had to live with that monster. She was going to be his prisoner. His slave. Or he would kill her. He couldn't just let that happen. He had to try with every single second, with every single precious breath in his body to escape. He pulled again, letting out a roar of effort as his muscles tensed, and his body bowed under the effort. He had such little strength left, and he gathered it all for this moment.

Something gave. Not much, but a little. His right arm felt looser. Maybe he had a shot. Maybe he could escape.

The canoe tipped. It had taken on a lot of water. It began to fill one whole side. It was going to sink. He didn't have time.

―――――

Liza

I break through the front door of the house. The long hallway greets me again, and I run down it, tears streaming down my face in spite of myself. I don't want to cry. I want to find Nick. I am terrified, but it's rage that's making the back of my neck hot and my stomach hard with tension. Everything is a blur. I have to find him. I have to find a way out. I make it to the far door and burst through onto the porch.

Everything goes dizzy on me. Just being outside, for only the second time in six months, is disorienting. My legs feel weak, and it feels like my knees might buckle. I grab ahold of the railing for the porch and try to steady myself. Deep breaths fill my lungs, and I try to focus on one point in the distance. I choose the rose bushes. My vision blurs in and out and then starts to steady itself. I feel like someone blew a balloon up inside of my skull. Purple spots are dancing in front of my eyes, and every breath hitches as I take a few experimental steps forward.

I don't fall. I have to keep pushing, then. I try to breathe deeply through my nose and out of my mouth. Walking more than running, I go down the steps and onto the grass. The feeling stops me. I can feel the grass, cut short and prickly, between my toes. I remember this feeling from so many times before, but to feel it now is exhilarating. It reminds me that the agoraphobia, what locked me inside that house for so long, wasn't real. It wasn't mine. It was all a story, crafted for me so that I wouldn't leave. I squish my toes down again, and the world seems to focus clearly. The fear of being outside is gone now.

Only the fear of losing Nick is left.

I look back ahead to the house across the street with the blue shutters. My feet begin to sprint toward it, and I am soon on the pavement. It feels wrong, but I don't have time to examine it. It feels more giving than usual. Springier. I make it to the house and pound on the door. The door opens beneath my fists, and I hesitate.

Stepping over the threshold, my heart catches in my throat. I can't comprehend what I am seeing. The stairs, so clearly seen from outside, they lead to nothing. The whole upper part of the house just isn't there. Each room, which looks so neat from the outside, only has half of the furniture in some places. An entire wall is just wallpaper, patterned to look like a countertop with a microwave and a stove and a window. It's a facade. The whole house is a facade.

I go back outside and stand in the grass to look at it. Again, something doesn't feel right under my feet. I look down and realize I'm not standing on grass. I'm standing on turf. It's fake. The neighborhood is fake. All fake houses except his. I run to the next-door neighbor's house and see it's the same. Frantic, I look around for something, anything that I can use to defend myself if he wakes up. My eyes find a pile of sports equipment by a garage door. A baseball, two mitts. And a bat. Never touched. Props.

I pick up the bat and run to the back of the house, stopping cold when I look back at the house that confined me. I am seeing the backyard now. There is no lake. No water. No area for children to play. Just a short yard with another small rosebush. So small it is barely a yard.

Everything was a lie.

"Daaaaaaaaaaaaaaaaaarling," comes a voice from everywhere. It's him. Alex. His voice seems to boom from every house, every street-lamp, every fencepost. "Don't worry, Darling. I'm coming. You won't be alone for long. Don't be afraid. I'll bring you home."

———

Alex

Waking up on the floor, blood trickling down his head, was not what Alex expected. It had been a long day, and this was just an ungrateful, disrespectful end. Not to mention the larger problem of Mary's apparent rebelliousness, just the fact that his whole day was nearly ruined was enough to set him on the warpath. He was going to go easy on her before. Not anymore. Her discipline would have to be much more intense. But it was for her own good.

And at the very least, for his.

"Darling?" he shouted to an empty house. "Great," he muttered, placing one hand on his knee to push himself up.

Blood stained his shirt, his favorite shirt, and he wondered if Mary would be able to get it out. Of course she would. She had nothing but time to work on it for him. After all, there was still time before Christmas.

Standing, he took a step forward and almost went down again. He wasn't even in control of his own body. He had lost some blood and stood up too fast, and now was woozy. She was out there somewhere. Maybe even outside of the house.

Pulling out the phone from his pocket, he opened the app his team designed for him to help him manage his sets. Navigating to the right option, he put the speaker to his lips.

"Darling," he said, drawing the word out long, "Don't worry, Darling. I'm coming. You won't be alone for long. Don't be afraid. I'll bring you home."

Even inside the house, the speakers boomed his voice out. He had spent a lot of money on those speakers, wiring them himself all throughout the soundstage before he built a single plot. He needed to be able to communicate with the entire town at a moment's notice.

"I'm coming, Darling. Just wait where you are. I'll be there soon."

Oh, the dreams he had, and the plans he had made. It could have been perfect.

It still could.

Yes, he had to tell himself that. All was not lost. Mary no longer had Nick to worry about. She was free. She just needed to understand that.

"Mary," he shouted into the speakers, slowly walking toward the doors. "Mary, don't go. You aren't ready for this, Darling. You aren't ready to be outside. Come home. I'm sorry if I frightened you. I just want what's best for you. Darling, I won't say that again. That was my one apology. Now it is your turn. Come apologize to me, Darling, and all will be forgiven."

He stepped out onto the porch, having made it through the double doors by holding on to the wall. His strength was coming back now. The cut had stopped bleeding, and he was no longer disoriented. Just angry.

He looked to the left and right, searching for any sign of her. The house across the street's door stood wide open, but nothing else was there. Then he saw the blood. Little droplets of blood from the cut on her arm. They lead to the house across and then away to the house to his left. Following the track, he stepped off the porch and toward the road.

"I'm going to find you. You have nowhere to go. There no point in trying to hide. No one out there is waiting for you anymore. I'm all you have. We have each other. Remember all our plans? Remember the life we're going to have together?

———

Liza

I can't find a way out. There has to be a way out. Maybe if I run to the end of the street, I can find someone...

Suddenly, it is daylight. Bright, blue sky, a sun bearing down, white puffy clouds floating by. The sudden shift was startling enough to send me to my knees, covering my head. The sounds of birds and cars driving by and children playing are everywhere.

Just like the mocking voice of Alex, they come from fence posts and gutters and mailboxes. It's not like the few moments I spent on the porch the first time I stepped out. The silence was palpable then. Now I'm surrounded by layered, intense sound.

Then just as soon as it came, it's gone. Night again. Stars above me. Soft crickets chirping. What the hell?

Daylight explodes. Everything is bright. Panic starts to set in. My mind is slipping. He was right all along. Then something catches my eye. A bird. A bird that seems to only fly in the same circle, over and over.

Nightfall again. Crickets.

Daylight. The bird. Circling, circling.

My heart squeezes so hard it sends a sharp pain through me as I realize what's happening. I'm not looking at the sky. It's a screen. Everything is being projected on a screen. I can see that now. That means I'm not outside at all. This is a soundstage. Alex didn't just try to create the perfect life inside the house. He created his own perfect world on a movie set.

———

Nick

The canoe was sinking. It was only a matter of minutes until it would be completely submerged. Nick's chin was just above the water, and he didn't know how much time was left, but it wasn't long.

No one was coming to help. No one was going to save him. He either could get his arm out, or he was going to die right there.

He struggled with the rope, but it was stuck. His palm wouldn't bend enough. Inches away. Inches from being off and he could untie the rest of himself and get out. Inches.

His body was numb. Everything other than his hands and his face felt like blocks of ice. He had stopped shivering now. His body was starting to shut down, and his mind had silenced its desperation for survival. It had given up and was just waiting for a quiet, gentle death. Most of him was underwater. Just his face and his hands and his feet were above it. But not for long.

The suspense was torment. Part of him still just wanted it to be over. To give up hope and die. But he couldn't. He couldn't do that to Liza. She had survived six months with Alex. He could survive a few minutes longer in the water. He tried again. The water rose almost to his mouth. He had to keep pushing. He knew he was going to die if he didn't. But the rope wouldn't budge.

———

Liza

I run to the next house, bat in tow. I have to find the exit. There has to be some way out of here and to the camp so I can find Nick. Laughter has begun to fill the speakers that are everywhere, but the day and night changes have stopped. I know the maniacal laughter is Alex, but it barely sounds like him. There is no control in this laugh. There is only chaos and venom.

I reach the next house and see the garage is standing open. I half-expect it to be another piece of wallpaper, but when I get close, I see something my eyes have trouble believing. It looks like a car with a rain cover on it. I run to it, noticing how bright the rims gleam back at me. I'd never heard or seen a car going down the road other than

Alex's. It doesn't seem possible this is real. But I can't walk away from it just because it doesn't seem real.

Yanking the cover off, I nearly cry. It's my car. Shoved into this garage as some sort of sick inside joke. A 2015 model compact in a neighborhood meant to be the 1950s. I almost laugh at the thought that I once felt like my car was old. Here it's a veritable spaceship. Alex was so confident in me never wanting to leave; he had tucked my car away a few hundred yards from where I was and didn't bother to take the keys from the ignition. That will be a lesson he'll have to learn.

Opening the door, I slide in, taking a deep breath, hoping against hope that if I turn that key still dangling from the ignition, the car will start. I close my eyes and turn.

It roars to life.

Thanking God for Alex's arrogance in that moment, I throw the car into first and peel out. Turning the bright lights on helps me see the walls for what they are. Solid cement, with a backdrop in front of them. Here and there are gaps in the backdrop, and I can see wires and cords and cement. I turn at the end of the street and see that the road just ends. There is a back alley-like area, but no more road. I turn down the alley, looking for any sign of a door. Any sign of a way out.

It hits me.

'Closer than you think.'

Alex wasn't just warning me that he would be able to get back to me too fast for me to escape. He was telling me what he'd done.

He didn't bring Nick to Camp Pine Trails or even meet him there. He created his own town, and I know in my gut he created an homage to the camp. Nick isn't at the camp; he's here. Somewhere. There has to be another soundstage.

'Closer than you think.'

He was taunting me, telling me he was going to kill my husband in the building where I already am.

My brights hover over the wall behind the house I had been imprisoned in. I can just make out a silver line on the wall behind the backdrop. It looks like a grated door. Like a garage door. All logic has to leave my mind. Now isn't the time to be cautious.

Revving the engine, I wait until the car is at maximum RPMs. If I am going to hit that door and crash, I want to hit it so hard I die. Otherwise, I am going through it to see what's on the other side.

I let go of the clutch, and the car roars down the alley. I hold my eyes shut tight as I brace for impact.

CHAPTER TWENTY-NINE

NICK

The water was rising, almost above his lips. The rope still wouldn't break, and his arm was weak, too weak to pull anymore. He ran out of time. He took a deep breath and thought about Liza.

Something crashed beyond the canoe, out in the distance where he thought nothing would ever exist again. Seconds later, he heard voices. He didn't want to trust himself. It must have been his mind disappearing.

One of them sounded like Liza. He took a deep breath. The water crawled up his nose.

———

Alex

Looking out over the lake, Alex could see the canoe almost under water completely. If Nick wasn't dead yet, he soon would be. Then Mary would be free, free to release herself of the burden of her former marriage, free to release Liza and embrace her true self. To become the perfect wife. His Mary.

She was still trapped in the town he'd created for her, for them. He'd go back to her soon and welcome her into his open arms. Disciplining her might be hard for both of them, but it would be what was right. Only good would come of it. For now, he needed to check on the progress at the lake. Julian was so obedient. Such a good helper.

Such a good scapegoat.

A sound crashing behind him startled him enough to make him stumble as he made his way toward the lake, sand from the area around the lake dug down deep into his cut, and he could feel the stinging of it pulling at his skin. Rolling onto his back to see what it was, he saw a car had crashed through the door that led from one soundstage to the other.

Her car.

He didn't care how she found it or how she found the door or how she figured out how to get in. He knew she would come here one way or the other, for Nick. Alex had only wished she would have a change of heart before she did. This would make it so much more of a hassle.

As it was, she was too late. Now she had no choice but to let go, become who she should be. He stood up, shaking the sand off his pants, looking at the car as the driver door opened.

Out she came, holding a baseball bat like some punk kid. This wasn't Mary. This wasn't what she was supposed to do. She was supposed to come see the evidence of all the hard work he had gone through to free her of her old life. She was supposed to be happy, to throw her arms around his neck, and be overwhelmed with relief that he saved her.

She staggered to him, obviously shaken by the crashing of the car. He wanted to go to her, to hold her and make sure she was okay. To chide her for being so silly as to crash a car. Instead, he stood rock solid. Waiting for her to come to him. She still had an apology to make.

As she got closer, she tightened her grip around the bat and narrowed her eyes at him. He held out a hand, palm out to her.

"Mary, before you do something you will regret, you need to listen to me."

She stopped several feet away, her eyes burning into his with terror and anger and frustration. He understood that. Of course she would be terrified, he reasoned. She was outside the house. Anger and frustration were obviously meant for Nick, and the danger he put Alex in by coming after her. She was clearly mad at herself.

"Where is he?" she asked through gritted teeth.

It made sense for her to want to know where his body was. It was the only way to know for sure it was over. Pointing out to the lake, he drew her attention to the canoe.

"Almost gone now," he said, a soft smile on his face. "He was so stupid to think I would fall for his trick. He called in a report to the fire station, knowing they would call me. I caught him just outside of the soundstage and brought him here. Now he is going to sink to the bottom of the lake and add to the story. The old camp is damaged, but this," he waved an arm to encompass the masterfully recreated set, "this is perfect. Welcome to Camp Pine Trails, Mary!"

Nick

The water engulfed him, and the canoe spun as the water filled it. Slowly it turned until he faced the sky. The stars were so beautiful. His eyes scanned until he saw the Big Dipper. His thoughts turned to Liza as he stared at the constellation and let out his breath.

Liza

I run to the edge of the water, but Alex cuts me off. I grip the bat tightly and prepare myself to swing, but he smiles. It throws me off, that smile. I want to bash his brains in and dive into the water, but the fear of it, even still, makes me feel like I am going to throw up. The water is where this all started when I was hurt, or so he said. In the lake behind the house. I know it's not true; that I was hurt while he was murdering Rebecca, but the fear still takes hold. It infuriates me that he still has that control. His manipulation hasn't been completely broken.

As if he knows what I'm thinking, Alex shifts his eyes and looks back toward the bay door. He points at it with one finger, a grin across his face.

"See, Mary? The house is just beyond that door," he says, and I look back for a second to see. There it is, the back of the house, right beyond the door, the house I was trapped in, where I thought I was someone else. Where I *was* someone else. "It's just like I said, Mary. The lake is right behind the house."

His mouth opens wide as he begins to laugh. It is a deep, full laugh, the laugh of a man gone mad. Everything I experienced over the last six months runs through my mind. Every indignity, every moment of being told my memories were of something they weren't. Every fake memory he tried to implant in my brain, all of it, and anger rose through my body. I'm angry for myself. I'm angry for Rebecca. I'm angry for Mallory. My voice, my hands, are all that's left to seek vengeance for all of us. I feel heat burning my cheeks. My eyes begin to water, and the hair stands up on my arms.

For the first time in my life, true, pure rage courses through me. I grip the bat hard and swing back, planting my foot like Nick had taught me one summer long ago. I step forward and swing out, aiming for that laugh, those teeth, that sound. The voice that had controlled me for too long. I want to kill that voice.

The bat connects, and a crushing, crunching, sick sound breaks the laughter. A sound like a half scream escapes his lips before the body goes crumbling down. His head bounces off the sand, and I contemplate hitting him more. Hitting him until the blood pools around the ground, and his brains are scattered among the grass. But my thoughts turn to Nick. The canoe is underwater now. I can see where the ripples are, where the air is still escaping, where he is drowning.

I drop the bat to the sand and step out near the water. I have to control this; I have to remember all that fear, all of the stories, that's all they were. Stories. I need to help Nick.

I take a step into the water. It washes up over me, sending an icy sensation along my skin. Without giving myself time to think about it, I dive in, pushing my body down into the water in the direction I saw the canoe last. Swimming until I have to try, I duck my head underwater. It's murky, but in a manufactured way, like a small amount of dirt was added to the bottom when the lake was built just to give the water the cloudy appearance. I can see ahead of me enough that in the distance I see a boat, now turned right side up, settling on the bottom of the lakebed. It's not very deep, and I swim closer, coming back up once for air.

Taking a lungful of oxygen, I dive back down, straight for the boat. When I reach it, I can see Nick, tied to the inside. My heart races as I realize he isn't breathing. No bubbles are coming from his nose, and his mouth hangs open. I swim to him as fast as I can and yank at the ropes that tie his hands. One comes off rather easily as I pull at the loop, but the other is snug. I struggle with it, pulling with all of my energy until it unravels. His feet are still tied, but they are much looser. Getting them undone, I grab his body by the waist and begin heading to the surface. My lungs burn, and I desperately need to breathe. I have been underwater far too long, and I am afraid I won't make it.

But I have to. Alex won't take us from each other. I won't give him the satisfaction.

I swim toward the stars above us, pushing Nick's head ahead of me, hoping to get him above water first. He needs to breathe. He can't die. As I get close, my eyes fall on the Big Dipper.

I push harder, and we break the surface of the water. Dragging in deep shallow breaths, I rest his head on my shoulder and hold him by the waist. I kick with what energy I have left until we reach the sand. Pulling him up onto the shore, I collapse on top of him.

Pushing on his chest, I do everything I can remember from the summer I was a lifeguard. Chest compressions, breathing into his mouth, more chest compressions, more breathing.

It goes on forever. Nothing is happening, and I am panicking. I am praying under my breath, begging for him to come back.

More chest compressions. More breathing. My entire body is shaking. Tears and sweat and spit and blood mix in my mouth and my eyes. More chest compressions. More breathing.

Suddenly there is a gurgle, a cough, and I collapse to my side as he begins to convulse and spit up water. A laugh escapes my lips as the exhaustion and adrenaline peak. I saved him. It's over.

Something pulls on my hair, and I try to reach up. Before I can find it, a fist crunches into the side of my face. Without warning, I am up in the air and being tossed backward.

When I land on the ground, I roll and see Alex looming over me, blood swirling across his face from his new wound. He licks his lips, and I see where he is now missing a couple of teeth. He looks down at me and spits.

———

Alex

Ungrateful, that's what she is.

When Alex saw her pull Nick out of the water, bringing him back to life, that was the last straw. No woman got to flaunt herself over him, not even his perfect Mary. If she had to learn the hard way, so be it.

He had thrown her to the ground violently, but that obviously wasn't enough. That wasn't going to fill the void the rage was making in his heart. He needed her to know just how much she disappointed him. Just how broken-hearted he was. He was going to have to hurt her the way she hurt him. He spit out a broken tooth, feeling around his mouth with his tongue. There were a few missing now.

"You have made a tremendous number of mistakes today, Mary. I am a very patient man. A very caring man. A very loving man. But you have gone to the very end of my patience. This ends now," he said.

Her eyes darted away from him, to Nick. He looked back and saw that he hadn't moved. He lay on his side, coughing up water, vomiting, and being generally useless. Like always.

"Leave me alone," she said, in a voice deeper than she used to address him.

It was sharp and modern and ugly. It sounded like trash coming from her mouth. He needed to shut that down, shut her up, make her realize that she was better than that, better than trash. Better than those ugly, modern women. She was the perfect wife. She had been so close to the perfect wife for six months. She would be again. She would be even better. All he had to do was prove it to her.

"What you need is a strong man, Mary. A strong man who can show you the error of your ways. I am that strong man. I provided for you when you had nothing with him. I gave you everything you could have ever wanted, and you spit in my face like some common whore."

"My name," she spat back at him, "is Liza!"

———

Liza

I rush into Alex, popping up onto my feet and exploding into his midsection with every bit of my body weight. We tumble onto the ground, and the sand fills my clothes, making it hard to stand and gain my bearing. He is up before I am, and he grabs my throat with both of his hands. I try to resist him, but he is stronger than I am, so I roll us over again.

Just beyond my reach, I can see the bat as I roll, and when we stop, I am on top of him. His hands close around me, but I swing at his face wildly, pounding my fists into the bloody mess that is his nose and eyes. I know he is having trouble seeing with the blood and my punches, but he tries to squeeze harder. I can feel my breath leaving me, and I have to reach for his fingers to pull them off. One of the fingers lifts up, and I bite down on it hard. Soon all of his fingers release, and he begins to pull at my mouth. I let go and scramble off of him, crawling as fast as I can for the bat.

I reach it and spin around. Alex is already on top of me, and I try to swing it at him. It lands in his ribs, and he grunts deeply but catches the bat under his arm. I try to wrench it free, but he pulls it away from me and spins it in his hand. Suddenly it is down over my throat, Alex pushing it down.

I try to hold both ends, trying to keep them away from me, but he is bigger and stronger, and he leans all of his weight down. Purple spots begin to dance in front of my eyes again. I can feel myself losing strength, losing the ability to fight. I can only hold on so much longer.

From above him, I see an oar, crashing down. It lands on the back of Alex's head, and he folds beside me, releasing his grip on one side of the bat. I roll out of the way, toward Nick, who falls to his knees.

"Run," he says, "I don't have much strength, but I can hold him here for you. Go."

"No," I say. "This ends now. With me."

I turn to stand just in time for Alex to push me out of the way. He cranks a swing off on Nick, crushing his ribs and sending him back down into the sand. I gain my footing again and jump on his back, clawing at his eyes. Blood smears all over me as I try to dig under his eyeballs. He yells and throws me off of him, the bat tumbling with me as he loses his grip.

When I get to my knees, I see the bat beside me and grab it with both hands. Alex is looking around his feet for it, one eye closed and the other bloodshot. Slowly his attention comes back to me, and for the first time, I see fear cross his eyes.

"Mary, put the bat down," he says, his voice returning to the measured, deep baritone I recognize from months of captivity.

"My name," I repeat through gritted teeth, each syllable a universe of its own anger and pain and hate, "is Liza!"

I swing downward this time, crashing the bat between his eyes. He slumps down to one knee, and I swing again. A sick squishing sound accompanies the crack of the bat on his skull as I hit him near the back of the head. His body falls, and I raise the bat above my head again. My mind is racing with a thousand indignities, all the little cuts and bruises in my mind that I suffered from his little game. One inexplicably wells up inside me, and I shout it down to him.

"And I hate Jell-O!" I scream as I crash the bat down again, smashing into his neck.

His body barely moves as blood begins to pool in the sand under his head. I raise the bat again, ready to keep swinging until there is nothing but brains and guts and blood under my feet; when a voice stops me. It is soft and soothing, full of love and sunlight and laughter. Nick.

"Liza. You can stop now. It's over."

I drop the bat to the ground and turn to him. He's only on his knees, but I go to him anyway, curling up in his arms and throwing my own around his neck. We sink into the sand together, and I finally let out the tears.

———

The police arrive only a few minutes later. Nick's call to the fire station was suspicious enough for them to try to send help, but they had gone first to the real camp. It took going back through his reports to the police station for them to know where to start looking. Nick stayed with Alex, the bat in hand just in case, while I went back to the house so the police can come there, and the ambulance to the lake set. As I walk back in, I leave every door open. I never wanted to be in this place again, but especially with a closed door. This time I have to be. Once the doors are open, and I have had a moment to make peace with what I'm leaving behind, I go back outside.

A few minutes later, I sit on the porch of the house across the street. Nick sits beside me on a chair, brought by the police who are swarming the fake neighborhood. We are both wrapped in blankets. Nick asks for coffee and chuckles when he gets it. I don't ask why. I don't care. He can do any weird thing he wants right now, and it will be OK. I am finally back to being me, and I am with him, and that's all that matters.

He leans toward me, and I nuzzle him.

"Babe?" he says softly.

"Hmm?"

"Did you just beat the hell out of a man and tell him you hate Jell-O?"

My mouth doesn't know what to think of the laugh, but I let it try to figure it out.

The bay doors I never saw are open, and there are police cars everywhere outside. The sun is beginning to light up the real sky, but the projector still shows stars. One of the uniformed women comes up to me and kneels down so she can be at eye level.

"Ma'am, I am Officer Torrance. Would you mind showing us the things you said were here?" she asks.

She seems nice, in that way that most police officers do after some trauma. She smiles a half-smile at me, and I look to Nick.

"You don't have to if you don't want to," Nick says. "I am sure they can find everything based on your descriptions just fine."

"It's alright," I say. "It's over now. I want to do what I can to finish this so we can go home." I stand and look at the officer. "Please. Call me Liza."

Home. I haven't said that before now, but it feels so good. When all this is over, I can go home, with my husband, my real husband, and take a shower and sleep on my own bed. I don't plan on moving out of it for a week.

Well, maybe on Christmas morning.

I follow the officer across the street and through the doors. Police tape has sprung up everywhere, as if it were a real house in a real neighborhood. At least they have all the doors open.

"Let's start in the guest room," I say.

When they are done dusting and taking pictures of the guest room, we move on to the study. I don't mind. I've gone numb.

CHAPTER THIRTY

LIZA

I walk through the house for the second time in a daze, my vision fogging up and occasionally having to hold on to the wall to stay steady. It's affecting me more this time than it did the first time, as if I hadn't really seen it, and now that I'm here again, it's tumbling down on me.

The officers keep offering to let me sit, to find me somewhere to rest, but I refuse. I don't want to be in this house any longer than I have to. I show them the crawlspace where the mementos were kept. I explain my dress on the ground and the clothes in the boxes. They take pictures from every conceivable angle, and then one of them with rubber gloves removes everything. They spread them out on the floor and go through each piece. One of them murmurs to the other one, and I catch snippets of the conversation, but I am barely paying attention. I hear the name Mallory once, but I can't place it. I never met her. She was gone before I came.

Next, they have me show them the study, and I point out the phone, still stained with my bloody fingerprints. There is a bandage on my arm now, covering the gash that will soon become a scar. Something to remind me of all this years from now when I am old and gray. As if I could ever forget.

"He had two lines," I say. "One for the house and one for the study."

"And you never called for help?" one of the officers asks.

Officer Torrance spins on him and shushes him.

"I couldn't remember anyone or anything. I was being told who I was, being told that I had these fears. He told me I was too anxious to get on the phone with anyone but him. I believed him."

Officer Torrance nods and jots something down on her notebook. It reminds me of Dr. Baker. They've already promised to go after him as well. He's just an actor Alex hired to pretend to be my therapist and then pass along the notes to him, but they'll charge him with fraud and impersonating a doctor. A good lawyer will likely get him off without any real punishment. That's fine with me. I have no place judging anyone for how Alex manipulated them.

I have already spoken to three other officers, giving them a testimony of what happened. I guess it was their job to try to find out the truth, even if it meant seeing if I would buckle under questioning, but I still resent him for that one and appreciate Officer Torrance all the more.

Before long, we are outside, and only Officer Torrance is in front of me.

"Mrs. Helmsworth. Liza?" she asks, her voice low and soothing. She doesn't want to rattle me or make me feel any more ill at ease, but she has to ask. "There is reason to believe there are bodies on these premises. You said you might know where?"

I nod, pointing silently to the rose bush in the front of the house. Yes, there is reason to believe there are bodies there. But they aren't just bodies. They are women. I watched one of them die and lay bleeding while she was buried. That is more reason than they will ever need.

"There. There is one under there. There is another rose bush around back, too. I would check there as well."

"Thank you. You can join your husband now. If I have any further questions, I will meet you at the hospital, okay?"

Forcing a smile, I nod at her. She smiles back and flips her notebook closed, heading back into the house. I make my way to Nick, who is standing now.

"They are going to take us to the hospital in the ambulance together, OK?" he asks.

Again, I just nod. I don't have many words left today. I might not for a long time.

As I step onto the bottom step of the ambulance, I see another one in the distance, back through the crashed in door, and by the lake. EMT's are carrying a stretcher, and there is a body on it. Only the sheet isn't all the way up, and they are tending to the wounds. Part of me wants to scream at them to stop. To just let him die, to leave him in the water, and let him drown like he tried to do to Nick. To put him inside the house and cement the door closed. To keep using that bat to bash his head until his skull is in a million pieces.

Instead, I turn my head away and step into the ambulance, sitting next to Nick and wrapping my arms around one of his. My head leans on his shoulder, and we rock gently as we are driven away. Out of the back door, I see the soundstage slowly fade in the distance, and I feel a twinge of relief. I will never step foot in that house again.

———

Alex

Waking up in the hospital was worse than being dead. Alex's head and body ached, and the nurses were decidedly rough and ugly. Rude too. Modern women. No more candy-stripers, just rough women with rough hands, never smiling, never doing their makeup, never taking pride in their appearance. He knew he would never properly heal if he didn't get to see a pretty face.

It took weeks to recover enough to even be questioned fully. Much of that was by his own doing, not wanting to bother speaking to them. But he could only pretend to fall asleep or rely on heavy medications for so long before he was forced to face the police. He sat in a bed, shackles keeping him from leaving, as if he could walk anyway, waiting for his skull to mend. They said his brain was exposed, and that he could have died if they hadn't gotten there exactly when they did. Too bad they did. Alex would have rather not lived in this world than not have his life. He had it all for such a short time. Mary, his perfect Mary. His house with the rose bushes. His study.

They had ruined everything. The plan was to tear it all down when the trial was over. The state was going to take the land, the camp, and all his assets, and distribute them among his victims.

Absurd, he thought. *I have no victims.*

They had sent him a lawyer, some moron with a stiff collar and loud ties. He thought he looked slick in his modern glasses and his spiked hair. He looked like a fool. He would get Alex sent down the river, as his mother used to say. Sent down the river to what, now that was what he wanted to know. To death, he supposed. Or to hell. Not that hell could be much worse than this.

He flipped on the television out of boredom and turned it off five minutes later. Nothing but sex and loud music and cartoons that aren't appropriate for children. The whole world had gone mad but him. All he wanted to do was live his perfect life, and no one would let him.

————

Liza

The trial took months to start, but once it began, it was even worse than the waiting. Suddenly, I have become a celebrity. 'The Amnesiac Housewife' or 'The Forgotten Girl' or whatever name each news station wanted to call me so they had something they could presumably trademark. I refuse to give interviews, but Nick does them from time to time. The media is something he understands, and he shields me from it. For that, I am grateful every second. No matter how much he tries, though, the story will always get bent and changed to fit some other person, someone who isn't involved, their version of what happened.

I feel like I should want to shout from the rooftops to set the story straight. Like I should want to do all the interviews and tell the world what a monster he was, and how the 'perfect life' was a nightmare. But I don't. I don't care what they say anymore, as long as I can sit there on the day the judge hands down his sentence, and I can look into his eyes, that's all I need.

Today is that day. I am wearing a dress for the first time since I escaped. Every court appearance before now, I intentionally wore slacks. I thought I might never wear a dress again, but when the jury came back after only twenty minutes to find him guilty, I changed my mind. I won't let him ruin anything for me anymore. Not one more minute of my life, not one more decision I make will ever be colored by him ever again.

I will take him down. I will dismantle him piece by piece. I will ensure he never again hurts another woman or sees the light of day.

And I will do it all in a dress and red lipstick because I fucking can.

I sit in the front row while the judge asks Alex to stand. With difficulty, either real or feigned, he does so, leaning on a cane and staring up at the officer. His hair is going gray now, and a stubby beard grows across his face. So different from the polished man he pretended to be. I watch him sag as the judge tells him how long he would be in prison. Life, on top of life. On top of Life. Consecutively.

Smiling, I stand up. Alex's head turns, and we meet eyes for the first time since my testimony. His mouth gapes open as he looks at me and shakes his head.

"Go to hell," I say, loud enough for him to hear.

"We all are," he shouts back at me, his lawyer trying to calm him, "the whole world is. This is not how it's supposed to be. This is not how it's supposed to be!"

I don't care to have the last word. I turn, holding Nick's hand, and we walk out of the courtroom. Reporters crowd around me for what must be the thousandth time, but this time when Nick puts his arm up and begins to tell them to go away, I stop him.

"It's OK," I tell him. "It's time now. It's over."

I turn to face the throng of cameras and microphones and bright lights. A smile crosses my face, and the words spill out of me.

"Let me start by telling you how much I hate Jell-O," I begin.

EPILOGUE

LIZA

Two years later...

Sitting across from Alex again is strange, but I love that this time, I'm the one who's free. At any second, I can stand up and walk out of the room, and he will still be a prisoner. There's a glitter in his eyes when he sees me. I resist the urge to shudder. He doesn't get that part of me anymore. He's not allowed my feelings of vulnerability.

"It's wonderful to see you, Mary," he says. I start to get up and hear the clang of his handcuffs against the side of the metal table as he tries to reach for me. "Liza," he relents.

I lower myself back down. In front of me, a tall, muscular guard has taken a step closer and is eyeing Alex suspiciously. They all know why he's here and who I am. None wanted me to come. They worry it will send him spiraling again. But I have to do this. I have to look him in the face and talk to him again now that he has spent twice as long captive as I did.

"You know the camp belongs to Nick now," I say. "It was given to us in the judgment."

"And my company," Alex adds ruefully.

"Most of it," I agree. "The rest was split among the other victims. Those who wanted it, anyway. That movie is never getting made."

The way his fingers dig into the top of the table and the muscle just beneath his eye twitches makes me smile.

"What are you doing with the camp?"

I shrug, leaning back in the chair and letting him simmer.

"Nick and I have talked about it. We considered burning it to the ground." Alex stiffens. The fear in his eyes makes me smile. "But that wouldn't do anybody any good. We offered some of it to Brian's family and to Mallory Maynard's parents. Neither wanted it. They want nothing to do with it. We'll probably sell it and let a developer turn it into a resort. That way someone gets to enjoy it." I shrug. "But who knows? Maybe we'll open the camp again."

"I hope you do," he says.

It's a plea, an attempt to reach for familiarity and connection. I lean toward him.

"That's the wonderful thing, though," I say. "You'll never know." I start to leave, but then I sit back down. "You were wrong, you know."

"About what?"

"You said it had to be treated as sacred ground because there was a body in the woods."

"Yes. And did they find one?"

"Yes. But you said they would find a woman. The detectives say they found a man's body. It took them several months to find it, but they think he died in December."

"Cause of death?" he asks.

"They couldn't determine it."

"Identity?"

"Not released," I say.

Alex nods.

"Interesting."

"So, you can let go of it now. It's not a special place with a sacred past. It's just an old camp where some horrible things happened. You have nothing now, Alex. Not your camp. Not your company. Not your money. Not Mallory, or Rebecca, or me. You have nothing, and you will never have anything again."

I stand and step away from the table.

"Will you visit me again?" he asks.

"No. I have nothing else to say to you."

I walk out of the prison and meet Nick outside. Filling my lungs with the spicy autumn air feels amazing.

"Are you alright?" he asks.

I kiss him long and sweet, taking in the taste of rain.

"I'm fine," I tell him. "How does hot apple cider sound?"

He gives a noncommittal shrug and sound.

"Good, I guess."

We wrap our arms around each other and start head down the sidewalk toward our car.

"How about at our own pumpkin patch? Because I've been thinking. We have a lot of land on our hands…"

———

Alex

Turning around and putting his hands back through the slot, Alex let the guard release him from his handcuffs. The cover of the slot slammed shut, leaving him alone in the stone cell. He climbed onto his bed and lay on his back, staring up at the ceiling.

Poor Julian, he thought.

He really was a good assistant and a passable actor. Giving him tiny roles won total loyalty. Alex was supposed to meet him in the woods at the real camp that night after he turned over Nick's boat and ensured it sank. Julian would never see him, though. The capsule he'd sprinkled into the drink he left for him took care of that within an hour after he left the soundstage. Alex didn't realize it would take so long for his body to be found. If it had worked out, Julian would have taken all the blame.

Oh well, at least now he will be remembered. He's the body found at the Cursed Camp.

But not the one Alex said would be there. He knew there was another one in those woods, one that had been there for fifteen years. But that was a story he would never tell.

CEDAR GROVE GAZETTE: OCTOBER 9

In the nearly two years since his arrest and incarceration, convicted serial killer Charles Alexander Whitman has refused to do any interviews. This changed recently after a visit from Liza Helmsworth, the woman who bravely escaped his clutches and was instrumental in his conviction. Helmsworth is said to have visited the prison for a short time last week, during which time she shared the details of the legal judgment against Whitman. In addition to his prison sentence, the judge ordered all of Whitman's assets distributed among those affected by his crimes. As a part of that, Helmsworth and her husband, Nick, a former employee of Whitman, now own his film production company and Camp Pine Trails.

Those familiar with the story will recognize Camp Pine Trails as the youth summer camp that operated for more than 50 years before closing down after the 2007 season. This was three years after a mysterious disappearance shook the entire Cedar Grove community. Whitman is said to have purchased the camp property just days prior to his arrest. The Helmsworths have not publicly discussed any plans for the future of the property but have said they are not allowing public tours or visits.

After the visit with his victim, Whitman apparently experienced a change of heart and decided it was time for his side of the story to be told. He reached out to reporters and has expressed his interest in a full interview. In his official statement, Whitman says he wants to tell the world of his love for another player in this complicated story, Lisanne Banes.

———

C urled in the corner of her sofa, Lisanne read the newspaper article again. When she was finished, she folded it and set it aside before finishing the mug of coffee she held. She stood and walked through the house to a large storage closet behind the kitchen. Taking out two duffel bags, a propane stove, and a blue sleeping bag, she piled everything on the floor in front of the back door, then went to the stairs.

"Jason," she called up. "Will you go into the attic for me and grab the tent? I thought we'd go camping."

He mumbled a reply, and she went into her small office. Sitting down at the desk, she took a letterhead and a pen with peacock-colored ink from the top drawer.

Dear Alex,

I NEVER KNEW...

THE END

———

My dear reader,
I hope that my book has brought you enjoyment and in its own way that it also brought a lot of thrills to your life.

If you can take a moment out of your very busy day to leave me a review, I would appreciate that enormously.
Your reviews allow me to get the validation I need to keep doing what I love and continue to pursue my love of writing.
It also helps me tremendously as a new writer just starting out.
It is always a challenging journey to start something new.
Being an indie author is no exception.

Your review doesn't have to be long, but however short or long you want.

Just a moment of your time is all that is needed.

When you leave me a review, know that I am forever thankful to YOU.

Again, thank you for reading my novel.

Look forward for my next one!

I promise always to do my best to bring you thrilling adventures.

Yours,
A.J. Rivers

P.S. If, for some reason, you didn't like this book or found typos or other errors, please let me know personally. I do my best to read and respond to every email at aj@riversthrillers.com

THE GIRL IN CABIN 13 (SNEAK PEEK)

Check Out Emma Griffin FBI Mystery Book 1 Now.

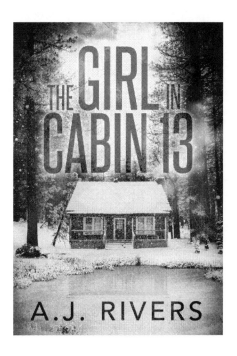

Knock...Knock...

When Emma finds a dead body on her porch with her name written on the dead man's hand she uncovers a sinister clue to the mystery that has haunted her since childhood.

FBI agent Emma Griffin is sent undercover to the small sleepy town of Feathered Nest to uncover the truth behind the strings of disappearances that has left the town terrified.

To Emma there is nothing that can lay buried forever. Even though her own childhood has been plagued by deaths and disappearances. Her mother's death, her father's disappearance, and her boyfriend's disappearance. The only cases that she hasn't solved.

Her obsession with finding out the truth behind her past was what led her to join the FBI.

Now, she must face what may be her biggest case. In Cabin 13 there lies an uneasy feeling. The feeling of her movements being watched. When a knock on her door revealed a body on her porch and her name written on a piece of paper in the dead man's hand. Suddenly her worlds collide.

With the past still haunting her, Emma must fight past her own demons to stop the body count from rising.

The woods have secrets. And this idyllic town has dark and murderous ones.

Either she reveals them or risk them claiming her too.

In Feathered Nest, nothing is what it seems.

The Girl in Cabin 13 is about to find out that the dead may have secrets of their own.

Order your copy now!

STAYING IN TOUCH WITH A.J.

Type the link below in your internet browser now to join my mailing list and get your free copy of Edge Of The Woods.

https://dl.bookfunnel.com/ze03jzd3e4

ALSO BY A.J. RIVERS